PREGNANT
ON THE
UPPER EAST SIDE?

EMILIE ROSE

Published by Silhouette Books
America's Publisher of Contemporary Romance

Special thanks and acknowledgment to Emilie Rose for her
contribution to the PARK AVENUE SCANDALS miniseries.

Starting over is never easy, but I've been fortunate to have
friends to help me through the transition.
You know who you are, and you have my infinite gratitude
for making the process as painless as possible.

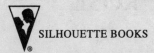 SILHOUETTE BOOKS

ISBN-13: 978-0-373-76903-2
ISBN-10:   0-373-76903-2

PREGNANT ON THE UPPER EAST SIDE?

Visit Silhouette Books at www.eHarlequin.com

Printed in U.S.A.

Recent Books by Emilie Rose

Silhouette Desire

EMILIE ROSE

Bestselling Silhouette Desire author and RITA® Award finalist Emilie Rose lives in her native North Carolina with her four sons and two adopted mutts. Writing is her third (and hopefully her last) career. She's managed a medical office and run a home day care, neither of which offers half as much satisfaction as plotting happy endings. Her hobbies include gardening and cooking (especially cheesecake). She is currently working her way through her own "Bucket List" which includes learning to ride a Harley. She's a rabid country music fan because she can find an entire book in almost any song. Letters can be mailed to: Emilie Rose, P.O. Box 20145, Raleigh, NC 27619, or e-mail: EmilieRoseC@aol.com.

Who's Who at 721 Park Avenue

6A: Marie Endicott—With her death still being investigated, the trail may finally be getting hot.

9B: Amanda Crawford—The favorite party planner is hiding something....

9B: Julia Prentice—Happily pregnant! Husband, Max Rolland, can't wait to be a dad!

12A: Vivian Vannick-Smythe—The stress of the building's landmark celebration and Marie's death is starting to show on the usually reserved socialite.

12B: Prince Sebastian of Caspia—Tessa Banks has certainly tamed this royal. Their wedding will be front-page news!

12C: Trent Tanford—The infamous playboy has finally settled down, and is pre-honeymooning with soon-to-be wife, Carrie Gray.

Penthouse A: Reed and Elizabeth Wellington—The long-standing couple has been acting like they're newlyweds again!

Penthouse B: Gage Lattimer—Ever the loner, he has been acting quite cheerful. Something—or someone—has gotten under his skin.

One

"Are you stalking me, Alex Harper? You're an attorney. You should know better." Amanda Crawford frowned at the too-handsome-for-his-own-good man standing beside the rows of mailboxes in her apartment building.

Alex feigned innocence. Badly. His coffee-brown eyes glinted with mischief, shooting off tiny gold flares in his irises, which in turn set off corresponding sparks below her navel. She clamped down on the unwelcome response.

He withdrew his hand from his black overcoat pocket and dangled a brass mailbox key in front of her. "I'm here to pick up Julia's mail. It's not all being forwarded to Max's place, and since I was going to be in the neighborhood I offered to stop by."

As excuses went, Amanda could almost accept that one. Julia, her former roommate, had married Alex's best friend just over three months ago. But Amanda had been seeing far too much of Alex to believe mail call was his only motive for turning up at 721 Park Avenue on a Saturday night at the exact moment she returned to her apartment building. No matter where she went lately he managed to make an appearance.

"The post office makes change-of-address kits for exactly that purpose. I'll send a few to Julia. Better yet, I'll fill them out myself."

Melting snowflakes glistened in Alex's dark hair, and he stood close enough that she caught a whiff of his cologne. She'd always been a sucker for Calvin Klein MAN, especially when applied to a tall, well-built body.

Stop it. You're all business all the time now, remember?
No men to divert your focus. Especially not this *man.*

At five foot ten in her bare feet plus her three-inch-heeled Stuart Weitzman ankle boots, she shouldn't have had to look up at anyone not affiliated with professional basketball. But with Alex she did.

"I'll take care of Julia's mail since I still live here," she insisted. "Besides, I have more upstairs."

"I'll come up and get it and deliver it when I meet them for dinner later."

Walked right into that one, didn't you, Amanda?

Disgusted by her slip, she turned and stalked across the marble-floored lobby toward the elevator. Henry the doorman sat in the center of the lobby behind his big mahogany desk, with the phone receiver pressed to his ear. She waved as she passed and his beady eyes followed her.

Alex kept pace beside her. "Why don't you join us tonight?"

"No thanks. I'm busy." Not exactly true. All she had

planned was an evening of combing her accounts and trying to find the money to cover her most pressing bills, but she didn't want to encourage Alex by accepting. Not that a womanizer like him apparently needed encouragement. She'd given him none and yet here he was. Again.

"When are you going to stop playing hard to get and go out with me, Amanda?"

"Never. And I'm not playing. I *am* hard to get. Impossible, in fact. So have a little pride and stop asking." She stabbed the call button and caught Alex's inspection in the ornate gold-rimmed mirror hanging on the Tiffany-box blue wall.

"I never give up when I truly want something. Or someone."

She attributed the shiver working its way up her spine to the record-breaking cold November weather outside the glass lobby doors. Alex's deep voice and the interest in his eyes had nothing to do with it.

"Especially when she's equally as interested."

She caught her breath at his audacity. And his insight. "For someone who is supposedly brilliant, you missed the mark on that one."

Amusement mingled with disbelief in his eyes. "Did I?"

Why bother to lie? He wouldn't believe her anyway. She ducked her chin into the fox collar of her cashmere coat and repositioned herself so she couldn't see him or his reflection.

She had to admit she found Alex's pursuit incredibly flattering, but she was smart enough to recognize a relationship train wreck when she saw one. In the dictionary of dating, Alex's name defined the words *temporary* and *heartbreaker.* Getting involved with him would be a disaster on a major scale. Not something she needed to add to her already infamous and blotchy relationship résumé.

"Why is it the party girl—"

"Party *planner*," she corrected instantly. Oops, that had sounded a little snippy and defensive. But he'd hit a hot button. Her disapproving parents had railed long and hard about her unacceptable career. If she heard *Get a real job or marry money* one more time she wouldn't be responsible for her actions.

"—parties with everyone but me?" he continued as if she hadn't interrupted.

She squeezed into the elevator even before the doors finished opening. He followed her into the car, crowding her toward the back wall. She put as much room between them as possible, which meant he literally had her backed into a corner. Not her idea of fun.

"Other people pay me for my services."

"That's what it takes? I have to hire you?"

"Yes."

"Good to know."

Trying to ignore him, she flipped through her mail and grimaced. Bills, bills and more bills. No surprise there. Her business, Affairs by Amanda, continued to grow, but unfortunately not fast enough to cover the balloon payment coming due on her bank loan.

If she didn't land a lucrative and highly visible event contract soon she'd have to consider closing her doors or—a fate worse than death—beg her parents for a loan to tide her over. Either way, her father would need a larynx transplant because he'd wear out his voice box lecturing her about disgracing the venerable Crawford name. Not that she hadn't heard that speech a thousand times already.

The elevator opened. She exited with Alex's shoulder bumping hers. The contact acted like a blaring alarm clock on every cell of her being. She absolutely detested his ability to affect her this way.

Honestly, the man had nothing going for him…aside from being rich, smart and gorgeous. It had even been rumored he had a sense of humor. But she could and would continue to resist his advances.

She dug her keys out of her Carlos Falchi python tote bag and shoved them into 9B's lock. It turned smoothly. The building might be prewar, but the security was modern era. If not for her friend Julia's connections, Amanda could never have found herself at such a prestigious uptown address. The real question was how long could she afford to stay without a significant boost in income.

"Wait h—"

"I'd love to come in. Thanks." Alex's chest bumped her shoulder when he reached past her to push open the door. The usual unwanted frisson of awareness hit her.

Why him? Why did Alex Harper have to be the one to ring her chimes?

She stared at him for five seconds, debated the wisdom of letting him in and then decided it wasn't worth arguing. He'd be gone in minutes. She left him behind and crossed the living room to the brushed stainless basket where she'd piled Julia's magazines and mail. When she turned with the bundle in hand, Alex was right on her heels. Her breath caught at his nearness. She shoved the mail forward, jabbing him in his flat belly, in an attempt to make him back off.

"Here you go. Thanks for picking it up. I'll show you out."

He stayed planted, his big body blocking her path to the door. His gaze held hers as he accepted the stack of letters and magazines. His fingers grazed hers. That fleeting contact hit her like a speeding subway train, quickening her pulse, shortening her breath and knocking her silly with lust.

And then he blinked his ridiculously thick lashes, releasing her from his spell. He scanned the pale pink and white high-tech decor of her living room. She could swear he zeroed in on each new addition. The votives, the trio of bubble-glass vases she'd picked up at an estate sale for next to nothing, the lime-green-beaded sari she'd draped over the back of the white sofa and the new raspberry tasseled lampshade.

"You've made some changes since Julia moved out."

"A few." He'd been in the apartment dozens of times, but not recently and never without Max or Julia as a buffer. Funny how he seemed to take up more space and air when it was just the two of them. "You don't want to be late for dinner."

"I have time."

She gritted her teeth in frustration.

"I want more than Julia's mail from you, Amanda."

As if she didn't know that already. Nevertheless the words sent a quick thrill through her. She'd considered *more* with Alex a time or two during her weaker moments. *More* would probably be pretty darn good with him considering all the practice he'd allegedly had. But the man and the timing were all wrong. She had to work on organizing her life before she could allow someone else into it.

She folded her arms and rocked back on her heels. "Really? Now there's a surprise. But there's this little word. *No.* N. O. I'm sure you're familiar with it since I've shared it with you so often."

The corners of his mouth twitched as if he fought a smile. She would bet a month's rent—which she didn't have to spare—he enjoyed their little verbal duels. Why else would he provoke her every time they met?

"You'll change your mind when you hear my proposition."

A proposition. Again, no surprise. Nonetheless, her mouth dried because she really was going to have to say no. Again. And each time it was a little harder to squeeze out that single syllable. "I doubt it."

He took off his coat and draped it over his forearm, revealing a charcoal Brooks Brothers suit, blinding white silk shirt and ruby power tie. "I need Affairs by Amanda."

He'd employed the one line that guaranteed she'd hear him out rather than kick him out. "For what?"

"Harper & Associates just landed a substantial public settlement. I'd like to reward the staff for their hard work."

He definitely knew how to tickle a girl's interest. A party for his firm could be good for business. His and hers. "What kind of event?"

"A couple hundred guests including friends, clients and a few celebrities to make it interesting. Choice of venue is yours, but I'd prefer something upscale like the Metropolitan Club."

Size and visibility. Class and clout. A-list guests who might be persuaded to use her services for their future affairs. Not exactly money in the bank, which she desperately needed, but the exposure could be just the boost her business required.

As a millionaire finance attorney, Alex had the kind of

connections she could use. Not that she didn't have her own connections. But his were better.

She knew there would be strings. A wheeler-dealer like Alex would always have strings. She curved her fingers in a "give me more" gesture. "Details."

He named a budget that made her salivate. "The catch is I'd like to do this within the month. The sooner, the better."

"That could be problematic." But a boon for her finances.

"If you're not up to it I can go elsewhere."

A power play. And he knew exactly what he was doing. She didn't miss the challenge in his eyes or in the angle of his chin. "What makes you think I'm available on such short notice?"

"Julia mentioned you'd had an unexpected cancellation."

A huge engagement party had gone kaput. The bride-to-be had run off with the groom's youngest brother. Not pretty. And while Amanda would get to keep the deposit to cover most of her losses, there would be little left after she paid the vendors and her employees.

She ought to turn Alex down. He was demanding and impatient and a workaholic like her father. He'd be hell to work with unless he stayed out of her way. And she doubted he would.

But she couldn't afford to say no.

"If I do this, your party is all I'm doing. Is that clear?"

One dark eyebrow hiked and his delectable mouth tilted mischievously. "Amanda—"

"Don't 'Amanda' me. I have no intention of being your latest accessory."

His slow, confident smile hit her below the three-inch-wide patent leather belt she'd cinched over her lavender cashmere tunic sweater. "But we'd be so good together."

That's what she was afraid of. He'd be amazing. Right up until the moment he dumped her. And she'd be left with yet another failed relationship. Wouldn't her parents love to rub that in her face?

"But as you pointed out, I'm an attorney. I know better than to force my attentions when they're not welcome. Meet me tomorrow to discuss the party details. Park Café. Four o'clock."

She sputtered at his pushiness. "That's less than twenty-four hours."

"Long enough for you to know if you can pull this off." He turned on his heel. His long strides carried him out of the apartment. The door shut quietly behind him.

She had her work cut out for her, but she'd be darned if she'd back down from the challenge he'd issued.

She couldn't afford to.

Amanda shifted her laptop case to her left hand, braced herself for another onslaught of Alex's charisma and pushed open the door of Park Café.

The upscale coffee shop was her favorite, and not just because of its close proximity to the building where she lived. If she ever had to have a last supper, she wanted it to be one of the café's double chocolate chip walnut muffins—preferably fresh from the oven while the chocolate chips were still gooey.

She waved to Trish, the barista. The warmth enfolding Amanda had everything to do with leaving the blustery outside behind and nothing—*absolutely nothing*—to do with spotting Alex unfolding his tall frame from a chair at a corner table.

He'd dressed casually for a Sunday afternoon in

charcoal wool trousers and a dove-gray cable V-neck sweater that made his shoulders look a mile wide. She caught a glimpse of the black T-shirt he wore between the cashmere and his skin.

Don't think about what's next to his skin.

Keep the meeting on a business footing.

And if he flirts, ignore him.

Easier said than done when even his smile invited her to break rules and promised she'd love doing it. Why did the man tempt her to throw caution and common sense out the window?

He pulled out a chair for her and nodded toward her briefcase. "You came prepared."

"I'm good at what I do. That's why you're hiring me. I brought a list of venues and dates that we can get within the next four weeks. Needless to say, it's a short list since the most desirable locations book up months or years in advance. I can pull up pictures of the spaces online since the café has wireless Internet access."

Trying to make connections with vendors on a Sunday had been absolute hell. But she'd done it by calling in every favor she was owed. This job was that important.

"I've ordered your usual. Trish said to tell you she'd start your latte when you walked in the door and a fresh batch of muffins would be out of the oven in five minutes."

Her usual? She'd met Alex here with Julia and Max a few times, but she hadn't realized he'd noticed she always ordered the same thing. Most likely Trish had told him. "Thank you."

She set her case on the table and extracted her computer. While the laptop booted up, Alex stepped behind her to help her remove her coat. Each touch, no matter how fleeting, hit her with a charge of electricity. Static electricity, no doubt.

Who do you think you're fooling?

He draped her coat over his on the spare chair. She sat quickly to get away from his heat and shoved a sheet of paper across the table the moment his behind hit the chair.

"Here are the sites, dates available, room capacities and prices. We'll have to act fast to snap up whichever one you choose because we're capitalizing on cancellations. Once we select the location we'll start on the menus.

"The Metropolitan Club is available for one day only, but I think the Trianon Suite at the Carlyle Hotel would be a better option. That time and date don't conflict with any of the other high-profile events going on in Manhattan."

"The Trianon it is."

That had been too easy. "Do you have your guest list?"

He extracted it from his coat pocket. Amanda took it and scanned the names. Adrenaline rushed through her. If she could convince just two or three of these people to hire her, Affairs by Amanda would be in the black for a long time to come. Alex definitely moved with the in crowd.

A shadow fell across the page. She glanced up and stifled a groan. Curtis, her lying, thieving ex, stood by the table. It took every ounce of civility she had to hide her less-than-happy-to-see-him reaction.

"Hi, 'Manda."

"Hello, Curtis. I can't talk right now. Could you please excuse us?"

The jerk didn't move. "I stopped by your apartment."

"Curtis, I'm working."

"Your balloon payment is coming due this week. Do you have enough money to cover it?"

Her cheeks burned. She did not need Alex to know she had financial issues. He might change his mind about hiring her.

"I don't have time for this discussion now. Later, okay?"

Curtis shoved his hands in his pockets and rocked back on his heels as if he had no intention of going anywhere anytime soon. "I could loan you some cash if you're strapped."

The money Curtis wanted to loan was probably her own. She had to get rid of him. "Why don't I let you talk to my attorney about that cash?"

She knew she was bluffing, but she saw her threat register in his eyes. And then she saw him dismiss it. His lips curled in a smirk. "Now, 'Manda, there's no need to get nasty. We both know you're not interested in making a fuss that would draw your parents' attention to your...difficulties."

Damn. Double damn. She glanced at Alex, and his dark, speculative gaze held hers for perhaps ten seconds. Then he shoved back his chair and rose.

She'd lost him, his business and her much-needed fee. Her stomach sank. Amanda racked her brain for a way to salvage the situation and came up empty. She grimaced an apology.

But instead of storming out of the coffee shop, Alex offered Curtis his hand in a friendly gesture. Surprised, Amanda searched his face. The hard glint in his eyes and his looming posture were far from amicable. In fact, she'd never seen Alex look so ferocious.

"I don't believe we've met. I'm Alexander Harper, Amanda's finance attorney."

Curtis's eyes widened. His mouth opened. The color

leached from his face and he winced. Amanda realized Alex must have crushed his hand. As soon as Alex released him Curtis shuffled back a step. He glanced warily from Alex to Amanda and back, then squared his shoulders.

"Curtis Wilks, Amanda's boyfriend."

"Ex-boyfriend," she corrected. "When you cancelled the lease on our apartment without telling me and then moved out while I was out of town, you ceased to be my anything."

He'd left her high and dry, and with a stack of bills. Since they had been splitting expenses equally, her name had been on all the utilities though not the lease. She'd been doubly screwed. She'd had to move and cover their debts. If Julia hadn't needed a roommate, Amanda wasn't sure where she would have ended up.

Curtis seemed to gather himself. "Yes, well, about that loan—"

"If Amanda needs anything she'll get it through me. Understand?" Alex's cold tone gave new meaning to the word *frostbite*.

Amanda blinked up at him. She wasn't used to anyone coming to her defense, and she kind of liked it. Even if he had lied about being her attorney.

Curtis took another step back. "Uh yeah, sure. See y'round, 'Manda."

Not if she saw him first, to quote the cliché. She watched him leave the shop.

"Pack up. I'll change our order to go," Alex said.

"Why?"

"You're going to tell me what's going on. And I don't think you want to discuss your financial status in a crowded coffee shop. We'll go to your place."

Having him back in her apartment wasn't a good idea. "I'd really rather not discuss my private affairs at all."

"If you don't level with me, Amanda, then our business is finished."

She sighed. What choice did she have? "My place it is."

Two

"Let's have it," Alex said the moment Amanda finished hanging up their coats. She hadn't looked him in the eye once since leaving the coffee shop.

She carried the bag of muffins to the kitchenette and fished around the cabinets for plates. After placing a muffin on each dish, she retrieved utensils and carried the lot to the small glass-and-steel high-top bar table. Her movements were deliberate and graceful, but he didn't need his body-language-reading skills to recognize she was stalling.

"Amanda?"

Her wary grey eyes finally met his. "How much has Julia already told you?"

Not nearly enough. No matter how hard he'd tried to pry information out of his friend's new bride, Julia had stayed closemouthed about anything that mattered about her former Vassar roommate. The only details she'd shared had been useless stuff he'd already figured out.

"Only that your split with Wilks has left you disinterested in a new relationship."

And Julia had only volunteered that because Amanda continued to shoot Alex down at every turn despite the obvious chemistry between them. He knew women too well to misread the awareness he saw in Amanda's eyes.

She ruffled her short blond hair with her fingers. The strands fell more or less back into place, but she didn't run to a mirror to check it. Amanda's lack of primping was just one of the things he liked about her. Her long, lean body didn't hurt, and the fact that she was confident enough to wear sexy-as-hell heels despite her height was a total turn-on.

"You heard Curtis. I have a banknote coming due and I'm running a little short. But that won't affect my ability to plan this event for you."

A wise man would back away from a company in financial trouble. But he wasn't feeling wise at the moment.

He shoved his hands in his pockets. "Do you need a loan?"

Her eyes widened and then her long lashes fluttered down. She focused on peeling the paper off the muffin. "I'll talk to the bank about an extension. Now, about your party—"

He wasn't going to let her change the subject that easily. "Spill it, Amanda. All of it. And then I'll decide whether or not we'll do business."

Her chin tilted in a defensive angle. "I am very careful about budgeting and planning ahead. We'll have a contract. You don't have to worry that I'll take your deposit and pay my creditors and stiff the people we engage for your event."

"I wasn't. But if you're so good with budgets how did the shortfall happen? Is business slow? I've heard nothing but accolades about your work."

She shoved her dish aside with a wistful glance at the muffin she'd crumbled into a messy pile. Instead of looking at him, she concentrated on wiping her chocolate-dotted fingers on a paper napkin. Stalling again.

"It's my fault, really. I made the mistake of allowing Curtis to help me set up the books and accounts for Affairs by Amanda.

"It worked well for a while. But then my operating capital started disappearing. At first I didn't notice because the amounts were small and I was too busy building my client list to pay attention, but then bigger chunks went missing. I questioned Curtis and he claimed I'd underestimated the costs of several major items. But I *never* underestimate. I always *over*estimate by five percent, just in case. When I asked for the receipts in question he told me he'd have to find them. Then he moved out while I was away for the weekend and left me holding all the bills."

Her case sounded typical of many others he'd handled. The embezzler started with small amounts to test the waters and then grew bolder and took more. "There are legal avenues for handling this situation."

"I know. But there are three reasons I've chosen not to go that route. Curtis knows them. One, I don't have the money to pay lawyer fees right now, and two, as Curtis said, I'd rather my parents not hear about this. Three, I may be convinced Curtis is responsible for the missing money, but proving it is another story. The questionable invoices mysteriously vanished when he did. And I had given him access to my accounts, so that makes me at least partially responsible."

His first instinct was to take her case pro bono. But he also intended to sleep with Amanda, and that was a conflict of interest he'd learned the hard way not to repeat. So as much as he'd personally love to nail the Wilks weasel, he had to hand this off.

He extracted his checkbook, a business card and a pen from his inside coat pocket. "I'm writing the name of one of the associates from my firm on the back of my card. Call him."

"Alex, I can't afford—"

"He'll defer payment until settlement." Alex would make sure of it—even if he had to guarantee the fees himself. "And I'll loan you the money to make your payment."

"I don't think—"

"You don't want to damage your credit by asking for an extension."

"Well…no."

"Do you want to let Wilks get away with this?"

"Of course not. But, Alex, you don't have to do this."

"What are your other options?"

She grimaced. "I could ask my father for a loan."

"You said you didn't want your parents to find out. Will your father hand over a chunk of cash without asking why you need it?" He barely waited for her to shake her head before going for the closer. "I want you handling my party, Amanda. If you're worrying about your finances, you'll be distracted and you'll give me less than one hundred percent."

And she'd be less likely to fall in with his plans.

He wanted Amanda Crawford for more than just sex, although that played a large part. Her networking expertise was unparalleled. The woman knew how to work a room better than anyone he'd ever met. She was exactly who he needed by his side to build the powerful connections that brought in clients and put money in the bank. She'd be an asset to his career for as long as their affair lasted, and it wasn't an ego trip to know he would be equally beneficial to hers. The fact that she wasn't interested in a permanent relationship only enhanced the attraction.

He opened his checkbook. "How much do you need?"

She hesitated. "Are there strings attached to the loan? I mean, do you expect me to sleep with you?"

Full disclosure wouldn't be in his best interest at this point. "When we share a bed it will be because you're tired of fighting the chemistry between us, not because of misplaced gratitude."

Her pupils expanded and her lips parted. "You sound convinced that will happen."

"It will."

"But you want something from me."

Smart lady. "I could use your connections. You introduce me to potential clients and I'll do the same for you."

She inhaled deeply as if preparing to argue, but then shook her head and blew out a long, slow breath. "I can do that. But, Alex, I never took you for the knight-in-shining-armor type."

Taken aback, he straightened. "I'm not."

Her lips twitched into a small smile and her eyes sparkled as if she had a secret. "I don't believe you."

A corner of his brain urged him to accept her change in attitude and use it to get ahead in the game. "Believe whatever you want. Give me an amount."

After a moment she did. He wrote the check and tore it out of the book. It was his job to get everything in writing, but discussing a repayment schedule would kill the deal faster than bleach killed germs. From everything he'd learned about her she would reimburse him. But if she didn't, he wouldn't miss a few thousand. And it wouldn't be the first time a woman cost him.

"Pay me back when you can."

Looking a little suspicious and a lot stunned, she took the check and business card. "That's it? You're just handing me money?"

"That's it."

"Thank you."

And then she surprised him by throwing her arms around his neck. Her body bumped his. He hugged her back, learning the feel of her lean length pressed against him, her breasts on his chest, her warm, smooth cheek against his and her soft hair tickling his ear. His libido howled like a wolf, but there would be time for that later. He released her the moment she eased back on her heels.

"Thank you again, Alex. I don't know what to say."

Her scent lingered in his nostrils. "Say yes to dinner."

She gasped, and her cheeks pinked.

"We never did get around to discussing the party," he reminded her.

She nibbled her bottom lip and then nodded. "Yes. To dinner."

Her measured tone said, "And only dinner." He fully intended to change her mind. But not tonight.

Success would take patience. And strategy. Luckily, he excelled at both.

Amanda couldn't believe she was nervous. But her damp palms were a dead giveaway. She pressed them to her flannel trousers.

Did Alex consider this a date? He'd certainly steered the dinner conversation away from planning his event, and he'd done so with such skill she hadn't even realized it until the taxi ride back. Each time she'd tried to stay on task he'd eased the conversation from the topic to people or places they both knew—people who would be at his party. Tricky.

Would he try to kiss her good-night?

Would she stop him this time?

He'd shown her a side of himself today that was different from what she'd seen before. She'd always considered him more ruthless shark than noble rescuer. Now she wasn't so sure she'd read him correctly.

Oh, please. Are you twenty-eight or eighteen?

As usual, Alex invaded her personal space the moment he entered her apartment. He stood with his hands in his coat pockets but close enough that she could see each blade of dark beard stubble and the fine lines in his lips. She yanked her gaze away from his mouth and tamped down the anticipation vibrating along her nerve endings. Her hands trembled as she unwound her scarf and hung it up along with her coat.

"Dinner was nice. Thank you."

The hole-in-the-wall Italian restaurant was new to her

but apparently not to Alex, who had been welcomed by name and immediately shown to a table despite the line of customers waiting to be seated. He couldn't have made a reservation because he couldn't have known she'd accept his invitation. She hadn't even known until the words had tumbled from her lips. And he couldn't have called ahead because he hadn't been out of her sight between her acceptance and their arrival at the family-run place.

"You're welcome. It's nice to share a meal with a woman who eats."

She flushed. She'd definitely done an embarrassing amount of that by packing away a salad, veal parmesan, crusty bread, her chocolate gelato and then some of Alex's pistachio.

"May I take your coat?"

"I'm not staying. Make the calls tomorrow morning and meet me for lunch to tell me what you've set up."

She scrambled to claw through her surprise or dismay or whatever it was and recall her calendar. Her Monday was lamentably open. She had a couple of small events in the works, but nothing more urgent than Alex's. "I could confirm by phone."

"No." Flat. Nonnegotiable. Bossy.

Her hackles rose, but she ignored them. "Where, then? My office?"

"Mine." He pulled out his BlackBerry and punched a few buttons, then slid it back into his pocket. "I should be finished by twelve-thirty."

His hand curved over her shoulder, strong and sure. The heat from his palm permeated her sweater. A shower of tingles rained down from the point of contact. He leaned closer. She caught her breath and swallowed the sudden rush of moisture to her mouth.

"You did a good job, Amanda. Your ideas thus far are top-notch. I'll see you tomorrow." His fingers tightened briefly and then he released her. She stood as still as a statue as he let himself out of the apartment.

No kiss? She stared at the closed door. She wasn't disappointed he hadn't attempted to kiss her good-night.

She wasn't.

This was business. Only business. And that was a good thing. Exactly what she wanted. She didn't have room for complicated relationships in her life at the moment, especially not with a finance attorney who probably thought she was a complete idiot for getting herself into her current predicament. She'd bet the trust fund she wouldn't come into until she turned thirty that Alexander Harper never made stupid mistakes with *his* money.

Tension poured from her muscles like sand through a broken hourglass. She headed for her bedroom, shed her clothes and took a long, hot shower. She conditioned her hair and shaved everything that needed shaving. She'd had to give up waxing to save the salon costs and because she was too much of a wimp to wax herself at home. She had a half-used waxing kit in the vanity cabinet as proof of her cowardice.

But the antsy feeling wouldn't leave her alone. Wrapped in a lavender towel, she padded into the bedroom, snatched up the phone and dialed Julia's new number. Her friend answered before the second ring.

"Moving pretty fast for a pregnant lady, aren't you?" Julia laughed. "You're just lucky I had the receiver parked on my mountainous belly. You sound out of sorts. What's the matter?"

She and Julia had known each other too long to miss the nuances in each other's voices. Julia heard Amanda's distress as clearly as Amanda heard her friend's happiness. "Go ahead and have me committed."

"Why? Are you dating Curtis again?"

"If I were that stupid I'd commit myself." She took a deep breath and confessed in a rush, "I agreed to plan an event for Alex Harper."

"And that's bad because…?"

"You know why."

"He's in hot pursuit. Yes, it's so tragic when a handsome, intelligent, wealthy guy wants you."

"Hey!"

"Amanda, you two can't keep your eyes off each other when you're in the same room. Max thinks Alex is a great guy. And I know you need someone to boost your confidence after that jerk Curtis. I say go for it—the party and anything else Alex is offering."

So much for her friend talking her off the celibacy-sucks ledge. "You know my goal. Get my life back on track and make a success of my business before I hit thirty."

"And come into all that money."

"I have to prove I can make a success of my business before then. Otherwise, my parents will just think Granddad's money bailed me out."

"Amanda, that's two years away. One brief affair is not going to set back your schedule."

"Says the woman who ended up pregnant after a *very* brief one-night stand."

"Ooh. You only fight dirty when you're running scared. Just remember Alex isn't the forever type."

"No kidding." She couldn't keep the sarcasm from her voice.

"In fact, he's quite a hound dog. Take precautions. You can't be celibate forever."

With her track record it would probably be her best option. "Why not?"

"Besides the obvious—that sex is fantastic with the right partner?"

Well, yes, there was that. "He's not the right person."

"You don't know that. Give the man points for persistence and reward his efforts already. Watching you dance around each other is exhausting me, and my poor, pregnant body is already on a hormonal roller coaster without watching all that longing in your eyes. Do him already."

She rolled her eyes. "You're not helping."

"Yes, I am. You're just not willing to admit I'm giving sage advice."

Admit to her newlywed and now aggressively matchmaking friend that she was attracted to Alex Harper?

Amanda would rather walk naked through Times Square.

At twelve-twenty-six the next day Amanda pushed open the heavy gold-stenciled glass door of Harper & Associates.

Alex's firm epitomized the affluent type of client Amanda longed for. Perhaps, she thought, she should consider targeting more corporate clients instead of focusing primarily on private affairs.

Her D&G pumps sank into the thick carpeting as she crossed to the cherry reception desk that had been polished to a mirror shine. A twenty-something blonde greeted her with a face and a toothy smile worthy of a beauty queen. "Good afternoon. May I help you?"

Amanda smiled back. "Amanda Crawford for Alex Harper."

"One moment please." She swiveled away and spoke quietly into a headset before turning back. "His assistant will be right with you. Would you care for a beverage?"

A stiff shot of something to calm her nerves would be good. "No, thank you."

"There she is now," the receptionist said, drawing Amanda's attention to a compact, midforties brunette charging down a wide corridor in her direction.

"Ms. Crawford? I'm Moira Newton. I'll take you to Mr. Harper's private waiting area."

Amanda followed her into a room that reeked money, from the wainscoting to the clean-cut lines of the leather and cherry furniture to the original artwork on the walls. If a room could instill a client's confidence in its owner, then this one would.

"Alex will be with you momentarily. May I get you anything while you wait?"

"I'm fine. Thank you."

"I'll take your coat."

Amanda shrugged off the garment, handed it over and sank into a deep wing chair tucked in the corner.

Moira hung her coat in a small closet hidden by the paneling, then sat behind a desk that fronted the remainder of her work space, which was discreetly concealed in a large alcove.

Moments later the muted timbre of Alex's voice scattered the butterflies that had been resting in Amanda's stomach. A door on the far wall opened and a harassed-looking, balding man stepped through, followed by Alex. As yet unnoticed, she drank Alex in as the men said their good-byes.

From the aggressive angle of his jaw to the straight set of his shoulders, Alex radiated self-assurance. His black tailored suit accentuated his height and athletic build, and his white shirt brought out his olive complexion. His dark hair swooped back from the side part, the ends covering his collar at his nape. Traditional, conservative clothing and furnishings, but the deliberately in-need-of-a-trim hairstyle hinted at a rebellious side. And her rebellious side snapped to attention.

Business only.

The client left. Alex turned and nailed her to the chair with his direct gaze. "Hello, Amanda."

How did he unsettle her with nothing more than a slow perusal and a *hello?* She had to work on shutting down that reaction.

"Alex." She dipped her head in greeting and rose, lifting her laptop case. "I have confirmations and contracts, and I need signatures."

"Come in." He extended his arm, gesturing for her to precede him.

His spacious office contained the same high-end furniture but had a slightly more relaxed atmosphere. A subtle hint of his cologne hung in the air. In addition to the desk and bookcases, he had a boardroom table set up in front of a bank of windows. He led her to that table. "Have a seat."

His knuckles brushed her shoulder blades as he seated her in the chair closest to the glass. She hid her shiver by reaching into her briefcase, extracting his file, then admiring the view of the Manhattan skyline.

"We have the Carlyle Trianon Suite for Saturday, the

twenty-second. We need to choose a theme and send out invitations immediately. If you have e-mail addresses for the people on your guest list I can also send out a blanket 'save the date' notice tomorrow."

He leaned back against the edge of his desk and crossed his ankles. His unwavering gaze pinned her to her chair. "Moira can give you the addresses. You look beautiful today."

Her brain tripped. She couldn't remember what she was supposed to say next. How did he fluster her so easily? "Thank you."

She dropped her gaze to the papers in her hand and struggled to regain her footing. "I have—" A knock at the door interrupted her.

"That should be our lunch. Eating in will allow us more time. I hope you like Greek food."

Lunch in an office shouldn't seem intimate. But it did. "A working lunch is a good idea. We have a lot to cover. And I love Greek food."

He opened the door to reveal Moira with a brown paper bag in one hand and tableware in the other.

"Need help setting up?" his assistant asked.

"We can handle it." He took everything from her, then placed the bag on the table and opened it. A delicious aroma saturated the room.

Amanda's mouth watered as he removed the lids from containers of feta, tomato and spinach salad, followed by farmer's bread and artichoke moussaka. He crossed to a small wine refrigerator tucked beneath a counter in the corner and returned with a bottle of Dry Creek Valley Zinfandel, which he opened and poured into two glasses.

She'd learned to keep a clear head when around Alex. "I don't usually drink when I'm working."

"The wine goes well with moussaka, but I'll get you a bottle of water if you prefer." He retrieved two bottles from a different refrigerator and set them on the table.

After scooping generous portions onto plates, he surprised her by shoving the containers to the opposite side of the table and sitting beside her instead of across from her. Their shoulders brushed as he adjusted his chair.

Too close. How could she concentrate with him touching her?

He lifted his glass and twisted in his seat. "To an enjoyable and profitable relationship."

"I'll drink to that." She lifted her glass and clinked her rim against his.

She took a sip. The zesty fruit-and-berry flavor of the cool liquid slid smoothly down her throat. She would have to be careful because she liked this wine too much, and that could get her in trouble.

Alex looked at her over the rim of his glass. "I'll need you to act as my hostess."

Her heart skipped a beat. She snapped her gaze from the food in front of her to Alex's. "You can't find someone else at this late date?"

"I want you, Amanda."

Three

I want you.

Alex's firmly stated phrase, delivered in close proximity and with direct eye contact, made Amanda's insides quiver.

He means for the party.

No, he means more than that. But you're ignoring the "more" part. Remember?

"I—I can hostess." Usually she facilitated events from behind the scenes, but it would be much easier to make those much-needed connections by Alex's side.

"I will, of course, cover the cost of appropriate attire."

God, he smelled good. "Alex, you don't need to do that."

"This evening will be as important for me as it will be for you. Buy yourself something."

Definitely bossy and not what she needed. "If I don't have anything suitable I'll consider it."

The hard look he shot her should have sent her scurrying to comply. Instantly. But she ignored it thanks to practice. She'd learned to deal with a similar look from her father. She reached for her fork. "This looks yummy."

"Aglaia's is one of my favorite places. Eat. Then we'll talk."

The salad was delicious, perfect in flavor and texture, as were the other dishes. They consumed the meal in silence. Unfortunately, the lack of conversation made it far too easy to get hung up on each shift of his body and each bump of his elbow, and it drove her to her wineglass more often than her water bottle.

Had she ever noticed he had great hands? Long fingers, blunt nails, sparse dark hairs on the backs. She couldn't remember experiencing this all-consuming awareness with anyone else.

Get a grip.

Finally, Alex forked the last bite of moussaka between his lips, chewed and swallowed. "Last night you said we had to choose a theme for the party. What did you have in mind?"

So he had listened before changing the subject.

He angled in his chair, his right thigh nudging her left. His heat penetrated the thin layers of their clothing and her thoughts snarled. She struggled to untangle them. Under the guise of shifting her empty plate out of the way she put an inch or two between them.

"That depends on whether you want a formal, traditional sit-down meal or something more relaxed and fun."

"Which do you recommend?"

"Your office is formal and conservative. If you want this to be a reward then I'd go for a 'festive drinks and

hors d'oeuvres' event. You said your employees worked
hard. Let them mingle and loosen up a little."

He reached for his wine, pursed his lips and sipped. She
found her gaze locked on his mouth again and pried it away.

You really must stop doing that.

She fumbled for her water bottle, hoping the chilled
liquid would satisfy her sudden oral fixation. The last
thing she needed was more wine. Her head was already
spinning, and she wasn't sure alcohol was the cause.

"Would you consider a masked ball? You could still
have a formal affair, but donning masks allows everyone
to let down their guard a little."

His left eyebrow hiked.

"Not full costume," she rushed on before he could
object. "More of a Mardi Gras in November. We could
even have New Orleans cuisine and music, if you like."

"Sounds like a good plan. Can you get a jazz band?"

"I've used a couple of good ones before. This afternoon
I'll call and see if either is available. Since we've decided
on a theme, I have invitation and decoration suggestions."

She reached for her laptop, booted up and then picked
up the paper file. Inside she'd tucked samples for several
different party themes in different pocketed folders. As
soon as he made choices she could enter the info online
and e-mail it to her supplier.

Alex rose and carried the plates to the wet bar in the
corner. When he returned he sat down closer than before,
his long legs bracketing her chair and his arm resting
along the back of her seat. His position hemmed her
against the table. If she leaned back she'd be in his arms—
one of the places she'd been avoiding for the past three-
plus months and intended to continue avoiding.

She fought to block out his nearness and focused on pulling up the images on-screen. "Here are sample schemes."

She clicked her mouse, scrolling through each page. He leaned closer. His breath teased her cheek and stirred the hair at her temple. Her mouth moistened and her pulse quickened.

"Stop. Back up." He spoke quietly, directly into her ear.

It took a few seconds for her brain to relay his words to her fingers. She cleared her throat. "This page?"

"Yes."

It was no surprise he'd chosen the most conservative of the bunch. She extracted a sample from the folder. "This?"

"Yes."

She picked up a pen with a hand that wasn't as steady as she would have liked and made a note, then did the same on the computer. "With that I'd recommend these."

She flipped to the next item on her list. Thank goodness the program she'd installed prompted her or else she would be floundering. What was wrong with her? She loved planning events. And yet today she could barely connect the dots.

Concentrate. "I'll make sure to order an assortment of spare masks for the guests who don't bring their own. Would you like for me to get one for you?"

"Amanda."

She turned her head at his low-voiced but commanding tone. Their faces and lips were scarce inches apart—the closest they'd been to date. The temptation to close the distance between their mouths streaked across her mind. She forced her gaze to his eyes and dragged a slow breath into her lungs.

Lambent desire flickered in his dark chocolate eyes. "You know what I want."

Did she ever. Her pulse rate rocketed. She swallowed and nodded. "I have a pretty good idea."

"I trust you to make the decisions to make it happen." Firm. Decisive. Not at all seductive.

What? Confused, she blinked and sat back.

"We've covered the basics," he continued. "I'll leave the rest in your capable hands."

Work. He was talking about *work?*

Of course he is. That's why you're here. Remember? Get your head out of the ozone, Amanda Crawford.

"I'll get right on it." She hastily closed her laptop, then grabbed the file folder and stacked it on top.

Alex shifted again, leaning forward so that his chest and arm pressed her back and shoulder, enfolding her in his warmth and scent. "Before you go, I have something I know you can't resist."

Her heart thumped like a bass drum, the beat reverberating off her eardrums and her gaze drifted back to his mouth.

He reached across the table and extracted two small boxes from the take-out bag. "Baklava. Two kinds. Walnut and chocolate. I couldn't neglect your sweet tooth."

She wasn't disappointed. *She wasn't.*

Yes, she was.

What is wrong with you? Do you actually miss him trying to get into your pants? How perverted is that?

But she was touched he'd noticed she had a weakness for sweets. Had Curtis? Had any of the men who'd blemished her relationship record in the past decade? Regrettably, no.

And what did that say about her taste in men and her

ability to choose them wisely? Nothing good. Which was why her sudden yen for Alex Harper was bad news.

She transferred her attention to the flaky confections cut into bite-size diamonds.

"Go ahead, Amanda. Dive right in. You know you want to."

Exactly. And that was becoming a big problem.

The police again?

Amanda's steps faltered on the marble floor as she entered her lobby early Monday evening. She hoped the police presence was more of the same old unsolved investigation and not some new occurrence in the apartment building.

As she passed under the massive crystal chandelier on the way to the elevators she nodded a silent greeting to Detective McGray, who loomed over the doorman's desk. His green eyes and lean, paunchy body looked tired and harassed.

The detective had been haunting the building since a former resident had been found dead back in late June. At first the police had believed Marie Endicott's death to be a suicide, but now they suspected foul play. The possibility of someone being murdered in the building gave Amanda the creeps. She shivered and shifted her attention to the doorman.

Poor Henry was sweating and mopping his face with a handkerchief despite the frosty air Amanda brought *whoosh*ing in on her heels. She couldn't blame the guy. The hard-eyed detective could make anyone squirm. McGray had certainly rattled her cage when he'd questioned her after the woman's body had been found.

Amanda hadn't even known the deceased. But she'd heard everyone in the building had been questioned. And then there'd been an even more uncomfortable Q&A in July when Julia had received a blackmail letter from someone threatening to spill the news of her pregnancy.

Amanda stepped into the waiting elevator. According to her former roommate, the scandals of 721 Park Avenue's residents could keep the tabloids busy for years. Yet another reason to keep the Curtis situation quiet. She wasn't ready to involve Alex's associate and risk exposing her predicament.

Which brought her thoughts back to Alex. As if they'd strayed far from that taboo subject lately. She sighed and leaned into the corner as the elevator shot upward. His enticement with the baklava had almost led her to create a scandal of a whole different kind. How she'd managed not to lick the man from head to toe right there in his office when he'd fed her a bite of chocolate baklava was still a mystery.

Kudos to her for having the good sense to invent another appointment and rush out of there before she devoured him and his baklava. Her willpower was stronger than she'd suspected. But it was worrisomely shaky.

The doors opened. She straightened and prepared to exit but stopped. Jane Elliott, penthouse B's housekeeper, stood in the opening. Amanda glanced at the floor number. Six. "Hi, Jane. Going up?"

Jane hesitated and then stepped inside and hit the button for the penthouse. "Yes. Good evening, Amanda."

The doors slid shut. Amanda briefly wondered who Jane had been visiting on the sixth floor and then shoved the question into the "none of her business" category.

She looked longingly at the housekeeper's long, curly

hair and wished—not for the first time—that her baby-fine hair would hold a curl. But no. She might have in-herited her mother's height and build, but she'd been cursed with her father's flyaway locks and pale coloring instead of the thick auburn hair and sultry looks that had made her mother a top fashion model for two decades before she'd traded in that career to become a successful clothing designer.

Bad hair. Just one more way to disappoint her over-achieving parents. As if she needed another way.

She shook off the negative thoughts. "Detective McGray is back in the building. I haven't missed anything new, have I?"

"I'm not aware of any new occurrences," Jane replied. The doors opened again. "Are you visiting Gage—Mr. Lattimer, I mean?"

Amanda's gaze shot to the numbers. "Oops. No. My mind was wandering. I guess I forgot to push the button for my floor."

"Good night, then." Jane left the elevator.

"Good night." Amanda stabbed the 9 button. The doors closed. She smacked a palm against her forehead.

Alex had taken over her brain, and she couldn't afford to mix business with her personal life again. It wasn't as if she didn't have a clear pattern to show her the error of her ways.

During her senior year in high school she'd fallen head over heels for Heath, the star quarterback. She'd almost flunked her last semester and that would have cost her her acceptance to Vassar if her father hadn't bailed her out by having a long talk with the dean. Amanda suspected there had probably been a deep-pocketed donation along with the discussion.

And then while in college she'd met Douglas at an art gallery. Talk about being stupidly distracted. She'd been young, naive and totally trusting. Douglas had been thirty-two, suave and so attentive. He'd swept her off her feet and taken her to Vegas. Instead of marrying her like she'd expected, he'd proceeded to gamble away the majority of the money she'd inherited from her grandmother on her twenty-first birthday. When the money had run out, so had he. She'd had to call home for airfare. Hadn't *that* been embarrassing?

By the time Curtis rolled into her life, her parents considered her truly stupid and irresponsible. And she'd proven them right. She'd been distracted by the whole falling-in-love myth and she'd trusted too much. Apparently her hormonal stupors caused her to miss critical details—details that still could cost her Affairs by Amanda.

But the hormonal stupors induced by Heath, Douglas and Curtis were like mild colds compared to the full-blown flu version Alex brought on.

Maybe a little inoculation would cure her.

No. Don't go there.

She couldn't afford to lose her business. That meant she couldn't lose her head. Because if she lost Affairs by Amanda she'd be forced to admit to her parents and herself that she was a failure.

"Alex." The flash of hunger in Amanda's eyes when she opened her door later that Monday was gratifying. The frown that followed was not. "What are you doing here and how did you get upstairs without Henry buzzing me?"

"I'm here because I heard you're a Monday night

football fan. And Gage Lattimer brought me up. He lives in the penthouse."

She gave him a patient look. "I know who Gage is. You took a lot for granted assuming I'd be at home and free tonight."

"I did, but I brought food, beer and fresh Krispy Kremes to make up for it."

Her gaze dropped to the bags in his hands. Indecision filled her face. She shifted on her bare feet, drawing his attention to her fuchsia-painted toenails. "I don't think—"

"And another party proposition."

He had her. Whether it was the donuts or the party that sealed the deal didn't matter. He saw capitulation soften her grey eyes before she opened the door wider, albeit with obvious reluctance. "Come in. But only if you're pulling for the Giants."

He grinned. "I have season tickets. Box seats. Fifty yard line. Be nice and I'll take you to a game."

That earned him a smile. What more could a guy want? Amanda was smart, sexy, a networking genius. And she liked football.

He scanned the place for competition as he followed her in, but he didn't spot any sign of a date. He had taken a risk showing up uninvited tonight, but his previous strategy wasn't working. He'd needed an adjustment. The exercise mat on the floor clued him in to her evening plans and explained her T-shirt, cotton pants and lack of makeup. Not that she needed to paint a face like hers.

He handed over the beer—an imported brew that Julia claimed was the only brand Amanda would drink. "Shove that in the refrigerator while I unpack the rest. The game doesn't start for an hour. That gives us time to eat and talk about my brother's birthday party."

His brother. The lie didn't slide as easily off his tongue with Amanda as it would with anyone else. For some reason he wanted to tell her the truth. He wanted to claim Zack as his son. But revealing that secret would cause nothing but trouble and could possibly hurt Zack. Besides, it was nobody's business.

"The party you wanted to discuss is for him?"

"Zack's going to turn eighteen in a few months. I'd like to throw a big bash, one he'll never forget. And I'll need your help for that." He shrugged off his coat and tossed it over the back of a bar stool before extracting the Chinese food containers and lining them up on her kitchen counter, but Amanda's eyes drilled the donut box. He handed it to her.

"Dessert first?" she asked with a wistful look in her eyes.

How could he deny her? If she would look at him like that they'd both be naked and busy. "Go for it."

She wasted no time ripping open the top, pulling out a glazed donut and biting into it. Her eyes closed and her head tilted back. "Mmm. Oh, my God, these are amazing."

Her throaty words hit him below the belt with a kick of arousal that nearly took him to his knees.

She'll look like that in bed.

He couldn't tear his eyes away as she greedily consumed the rest of her prize. She didn't lift her lids until she'd finished the last sugary bite. Her tongue swept her lips, but white flakes of glaze clung to the corners. She lifted one finger to her mouth and licked.

He wanted that job.

Screw strategy. He grabbed her hand, carried it to his

mouth and lapped her sticky fingertip with his tongue. Her breath hitched. But she didn't slap him or yank her hand away. Without taking his eyes off hers he moved from the first sweetened digit to the second. His tongue swirled around the tip, and then he pulled her thumb into his mouth and repeated the process. Her pupils dilated and her lips parted.

He had to have her mouth. Now. Releasing her hand, he closed the distance between them.

"You have more sugar here." He dipped his head to lick it away.

She leaned into him, lifting her chin in silent invitation. She didn't have to ask twice. He traced the sugary outline of her lips. It wasn't enough. He covered her mouth with his and delved into her silky warmth. The sweetness of the donut gave way to the unique flavor of the woman in his arms.

He'd been waiting months for this. He caught her waist and pulled her closer, crushing her against his chest and deepening the kiss. Her hands rested briefly on his shoulders, her short nails digging into his muscles and then her arms slid around his neck. She opened her mouth wider for him and her tongue sought his, slick and sweet, warm and wet.

She fit against him even better than he'd expected. Need rumbled up from his gut to his throat. He mapped her spine, her waist, her hips. She was long and lean and hot. His fingers found silky bare skin between the hem of her shirt and the waistband of her pants.

She gasped and lifted her head. But she didn't pull away. Her passion-darkened eyes sought his. "I— We shouldn't do this, Alex."

"It's long overdue."

Her gaze dropped back to his mouth. Regret flickered across her face. "I don't sleep with my clients."

"Should I fire you?" he teased.

She stiffened and panic widened her eyes. "You'd do that?"

He rubbed her back soothingly, enjoying the smooth warmth of her skin. "No. I honor my promises. And I promise you, Amanda, this isn't a mistake. We're going to be magnificent together. In bed *and* out."

Indecision flitted across her features. And then she sighed. Her fingers threaded through his hair. She pulled his face back to hers. Whatever he'd expected, it wasn't the aggressive, carnal, no-holds-barred kiss she planted on him.

She devoured him with the same intensity she'd given to the baklava at lunch and the donut tonight, and he was more than willing to be consumed. He cupped her butt and pressed her hips to his. If she hadn't known where he wanted this to go then his growing erection was a dead giveaway. Damn, she was potent.

By the time she lifted her head and slid her hands to his pectorals, his heart was slamming like a wrecking ball against his chest wall.

She licked her damp lips. "This is crazy. I don't have time for a man in my life right now. For the next few years, my career is my priority. Alex, if you can't handle this being temporary then we need to stop. Now."

Her frankness momentarily took him aback. But her willingness to speak freely was one of the things he liked about Amanda. Was she joking? What man would say no to a brief, passionate affair? Temporary was his specialty.

"I can handle it. Where's your bedroom?"

For a second she hesitated, looking as if she might change her mind, but then she took his hand and led him across the living room. His gaze dropped to her butt in the thin knit pants. Nice. Firm. Rounded.

Her bedroom was as pink and white and feminine as the rest of the apartment. A thick, white faux-fur rug covered the floor. Filmy white drapes, tied back with brightly colored silky-looking scarves, hung behind a platform bed in a makeshift headboard. He'd never been one for bondage, but he couldn't help thinking those scarves could come in handy later. He would like to tie her up and pleasure her until she begged him to stop.

Right now he was too impatient to play sexy games.

He yanked her hand, spinning her back into his arms. Their bodies and mouths slammed together, lips parting, tongues clashing. She met him stroke for stroke. Her fingers dug into his waist. Her pelvis nudged his. She wasn't shy or coy, and her boldness was an incredible turn-on. He whisked her shirt over her head. Before he could savor her pale, smooth skin she attacked his shirt without hesitation.

Dressed, Amanda looked deceptively lean, but she had curves. Not overblown. But subtle, exquisite. Perfect. He wanted to linger, to savor her breasts above her lavender lace bra, but he'd wanted Amanda for months and hunger snuffed out patience. The bra gave way with a flick of his fingers. He tossed it aside and caught one puckered pink nipple in his mouth, the other in his hand. She tasted good. Smelled good. Her pale skin was warm and silky soft against his lips.

Her fingers speared his hair, flexed into his scalp with an energizing tug. Then she lightly scraped her nails across his shoulders and down his sides. His muscles rippled in the wake of her touch. Her nimble fingers encountered his belt. The leather gave way quickly, followed by the button and zipper of his pants. She had him so aroused he could barely concentrate.

Apparently he wasn't the only one in a hurry. Her palms flattened against his hips and shoved the fabric of his pants and boxers over his butt and down his thighs. Her caress sent a shock of need through him, making him grit his teeth and struggle to fill his lungs.

He released her long enough to kick off his shoes and the remainder of his clothing, and then he ripped her pants down her long legs. The tattoo he uncovered when he removed her bikini panties caught him by surprise. "A martini?"

She nibbled her bottom lip as if she expected him to be repulsed by the ink. "An appletini. It's a reminder that life's supposed to be fun."

With one finger he outlined the tilted glass just below her left hipbone and then knelt and sipped from the inked rim. He lifted his gaze to hers and rose. "It's sexy as hell. Tasty, too."

Her slow smile and the desire in her eyes decimated what was left of his control. "So are you."

And that's when he realized he might be in trouble. A little of Amanda Crawford might not be enough.

Four

Alexander Harper had been hiding a body to die for beneath his custom designer suits.

His wide shoulders, ropey muscles and washboard abs had Amanda salivating for the feel of those brawny arms wrapped around her. She bisected his smooth chest with her fingers, drawing a line between his pectorals to the goody trail below his navel and the dense dark hair surrounding his erection. His stomach quivered beneath her touch and his arousal twitched, begging her to curl her fingers around his thick length. She wasted no time in doing so. His breath whistled.

"Amanda." The man actually growled.

She grinned mischievously up at him and stroked him from base to tip. "Yes?"

His pupils expanded and his skin flushed. "You're playing with fire."

"That's okay. I like it hot." She just hoped her desire for Alex didn't burn her before it burned out.

Experience told her this was a mistake, but she couldn't stop now. He'd monopolized her thoughts for three long months and she ached for him. Her thumb found a slick droplet pearling on his engorged tip and spread it around. She leaned forward to lick his tiny, brown nipple.

One strong arm banded around her, yanking her flush against his hot torso. His other hand stabbed into her hair, fisted and tugged just hard enough to force her head back. The combination of his scorching heat, his strength and his controlled aggression robbed her breath. His kiss was hard, bordering on rough, his passion barely contained. And she loved it. How long had it been since anyone wanted her so intensely? Had anyone, ever? She couldn't remember. But she doubted it.

She released his erection, wound her arms around his neck and relished the heady desire racing through her. She loved that Alex was taller and broader than she. Both Curtis and Douglas had been her height. She'd felt like an Amazon with them. But not with Alex. He was bigger in *every* way, and he loomed over her, making her feel dainty, desirable and feminine and not the least bit delicate.

He skimmed her curves, kneaded her bottom. His tongue and hands worked magic, arousing her beyond anything she'd ever experienced as they flexed into her flesh. She kissed him back, tangling her fingers in his hair and arching as tight against him as she could get. It wasn't close enough. She wanted to wind herself around him but settled for lifting her leg, sliding it up the outside of his hair-roughened, rock-hard, muscled thigh and hooking it around his waist. He grasped her knee and arched his hips, plunging deep inside her. The shock of his sudden penetration filled her, forcing the breath from her lungs on a moan of pure ecstasy.

He withdrew and then rocked upward again and again, nearly lifting her off the ground with each thrust. Her heart raced and every muscle in her body clenched with need as he drove deep, so deep inside her.

Alex swung her around and her world tilted. She felt herself falling. She clung to his shoulders and whimpered into his mouth, but he didn't drop her. He eased her onto the mattress. Cool sheets pressed against her back, but it was the hot body above her and driving into her that held her rapt attention.

She tore her mouth free to gasp for air and buried her face in his neck. She couldn't resist a nibble. He smelled good, tasted good, felt good. Around her. Over her. Inside her. Tension coiled below her navel. She squeezed him tight internally and externally, clasped his tight buttocks and pulled him in deeper still.

His groan reverberated against her chest. With each thrust he teased exactly the right spot, and she was getting close, so close. He captured her shoulders and barrel-rolled them sideways until he was on his back and she straddled him on her knees.

"Finish us," he ordered hoarsely. His hand found her breasts.

She'd never been much for taking orders, but when he tweaked her nipples like that, sending darts of pleasure straight to her core, she would do pretty much anything he asked. She rose above him and then sank down, taking as much of him as she could. Over and over she filled herself with him, rose and dropped, swiveled and rocked. Again and again. His blunt-cut nails raked down her belly to comb through her pale curls. He found her center and buffed her with his thumb.

She wanted to wait, to savor, to explore the tension twisting tighter with each caress, but it had been too long. She couldn't hold off. Ecstasy exploded through her, radiating outward in shock wave after shock wave. Her muscles contracted, whipping her forward until she and Alex were face to face, breast to breast, her palms planted beside his head. She lost herself in the hunger burning in his eyes, hunger for her that beat anything she'd experienced before. He gripped her hips as he thrust upward, harder and faster, and then his eyes squeezed shut and his body bowed off the bed as release jerked through him, setting off a series of tiny aftershocks inside her.

Their rapid breaths mingled as she stared at the handsome face beneath hers and tried to right her world. She'd had sex with demanding, impatient, workaholic Alex Harper. And she was absolutely certain she was going to regret that…in a minute.

But right now she felt too damned good to worry that Alex Harper had just given her the best sex of her life.

Alex Harper was a *god* in bed. Amanda could have lived without that knowledge.

Muscles quivering, she fell back on her pillow and stared at the ceiling, trying to catch her breath and listening to Alex doing the same beside her. Wow.

The road to hell was paved with good intentions. And she had paved miles of it last night. She'd meant to send Alex packing the second he'd arrived. But the fresh, still warm donuts, along with the possibility of another party contract, had defeated her.

And then she'd meant to kick him out when he licked her fingers, igniting a blaze inside her. But she hadn't been able to say the words *no* or *go*.

She'd planned to send him home after they made love the first time. And again after the second. But somehow they'd ended up sharing dinner while watching the second half of the Giants game *naked* before climbing back into bed, where he'd held her until she'd fallen asleep.

Third time the charm? Could she rally her willpower this time? And did she really want to?

Starting a Tuesday morning with multiple orgasms beat an alarm clock any day of the week. She smiled to herself and turned her head to find Alex's dark eyes focused on her.

Her heart skipped a beat. Having him here felt too good. Too right. "You should go."

"In a minute. Right now I don't think I could stand." He delivered the words with a rueful but naughty smile that practically turned her wrong-side-outward.

The scent of their lovemaking permeated her bedroom. The lingering fatigue of a busy night weighted her muscles. Amanda wasn't sure she had the strength to crawl to the shower and prepare for her morning appointment. Alex had even farther to go.

"How will you make it to Connecticut and back in time for work?"

"I keep a spare suit at the office. I'll shower here. With you."

A thrill raced through her, but she choked out a laugh. "I don't have to be psychic to know how that'll end up. With both of us being late for work."

He grinned and rolled onto his side. But then his smile faded. He gently brushed the hair off her cheek and tucked it behind her ear. "Come home with me this weekend."

Her lungs refused to work.

"We never discussed Zack's party. He's a great kid. If you meet him you'll get a feel for what he likes, and we'll have a better chance of surprising him with something that'll blow his mind."

Work. He's talking about work. Focus. "You want this to be a surprise party?"

"Yes. Spend the weekend at my place. You can meet Zack and my parents."

She recoiled. The last thing she needed was for her mom and dad to get wind of her dating Alex. He would be the only man she'd ever hooked up with that they would consider suitable. And she was throwing him back just as soon as she came to her senses.

"Alex, we don't have and will never have a meet-the-parents kind of relationship."

He shook his head. "That's not what I'm implying. You need to visit my parents' house. That's probably the best place for the party if we want to keep it under wraps. If after you see the place you don't like that idea, then I'd like to have the party somewhere else in Greenwich so Zack's friends can come. You'll have to help me choose an alternate location."

Why did he keep making offers she couldn't afford to refuse? She sighed. "If I say yes to spending the weekend with you, you're not going to take it the wrong way and think this affair is more than temporary insanity, are you?"

He rolled over her, planting his knees between hers and propping his elbows on either side of her body. His eyes held hers and his breath teased her lips. Desire stirred anew. "This relationship will last only as long as it's beneficial to both of us."

And with his body intimately connected to hers it was hard not to appreciate the benefits of their association. But uncertainty nagged her, tensing muscles that had been completely lax just moments ago.

She forced herself to relax. She needed this job and any other that Alex could throw her way. She could handle whatever else came up. And he was hellaciously good in bed.

"Okay. I'll come to Greenwich with you."

Amanda had known Alex was loaded, but she hadn't expected his home to be a large estate at the end of a winding, white-fenced, paddock-lined road in the Greenwich backcountry.

She followed him into the sprawling stone center hall colonial Friday evening and paused in the two-storied marbled and wainscoted foyer. To her left she could see a living room with a soaring stone fireplace, a wet bar and a suede sectional sofa.

"Alex, this is nice."

"Were you expecting a bachelor pad?"

She wrinkled her nose. "You do have a reputation as a guy with a short attention span."

"Is that why you kept playing hard to get?"

"I told you I wasn't playing. I *am* hard to get. Not that you'd know it by this week's performance."

His lips tilted in that sexy, I'm-going-to-get-you-in-trouble-and-you're-going-to-love-it smile that made her insides hum like a beehive. He set their bags at the foot of the stairs and strolled toward her, lazily, but with a predatory glint in his eyes that quickened her pulse. "I have no complaints with your performance."

Her body flushed from her center to her fingertips, which she pressed to his chest to stop the embrace she saw coming. "Nor I yours, but we'll never get the details of your party finalized if you don't quit distracting me."

Alex had come to her place two of the past three evenings after work under the guise of planning his party. He'd spent the nights, but not working on arrangements. She hadn't started regretting the involvement yet. But she knew she would. Her relationships always came back to bite her.

He captured her hand with his, lacing their fingers. "I'll give you a quick tour."

"Don't we have to be at your parents' for dinner soon?"

Mischief glinted in his eyes. She'd seen that look often enough recently to know it meant he wanted her naked, and if she gave him about three seconds' leeway she'd want it, too. Anticipation made her pulse stutter.

"That's why you're getting the abbreviated tour. Otherwise I'd be showing you my bedroom from beneath the sheets. You wouldn't see much of the house that way." The man oozed sexuality.

Desire pulsed through her. She tamped it down. "Lead on."

Her heels tapped out a beat on the hardwood floors as he whisked her past a cherry-paneled study, formal living and dining rooms and through the gourmet eat-in kitchen with black-granite countertops. The place begged for a family to fill it and for a woman to soften the stark decor with a vase of flowers here and there or a few knickknacks or framed photographs.

Did Alex plan to marry and have children? She'd never heard of him staying with anyone long enough to get close to settling down. But why own a place like this if he didn't plan to start a family?

And why do you care?

You don't.

She followed him outside onto a limestone-tile patio. Her breath clouded the cold night air. Outdoor lighting illuminated a lap pool that had to be at least fifty feet long. In the shadows beyond the subtle glow she caught hints of lawn and in the distance a low stone wall like the one out front. Evergreen trees mingled with the bare-limbed deciduous variety—one of which had a huge branch perfect for a rope swing. Alex's home would be the perfect place to raise children.

Children. She'd never thought about having them. And couldn't now. Her life was a mess. Until she had that straightened out, she couldn't think about adding complications. But she suddenly wondered if she was missing out.

Of course not. What do you know about good parenting? Nada.

She hugged her coat tighter around her to ward off the frosty air. "You said bring a swimsuit, but it's too cold to swim."

"I have a hot tub if you want to brave it later." He pointed toward a sheltered corner of the patio. "But my parents have an indoor pool. Tomorrow we can swim with Zack, and you can try to get a feel for what kind of party he'd like."

He led her back inside and up the stairs to a vaulted-ceiling bedroom decorated in black, white and grey. A king-size bed with a raw-silk pewter bedspread and a massive, carved cherry headboard took up only a quarter of the large room. A gas fireplace with a cozy sitting area had been centered on the wall opposite the bed, and French doors led to a Juliet balcony overlooking the pool and large backyard. She suspected the view from the windows would be beautiful and green in summer.

The room reminded her of Alex. Luxurious, but no frills, no clutter.

Her gaze returned to the bed she'd be sharing with him. It didn't bother her that she'd be just one of many to pass through it.

It didn't.

Yes, it did. And that made no sense. She had no claim on him. And didn't want one.

"Is this where you entertain your women?" She wanted the catty words back the instant she said them. Why had she said them? She wasn't usually the type to blurt out her thoughts.

"I don't bring women here. I go to their place. You might have noticed the express-train commute and climbing into a cold car at the depot isn't exactly romantic." Alex left his Mercedes at the station every day before heading for Manhattan.

She smiled. "I can see how a forty-minute ride on the express train could kill the mood."

He stroked a fingertip along her jaw, sending ripples of arousal through her. "Has it killed the mood?"

Not even close. She would much rather stay here, strip down and make love with him in front of a roaring fire than eat with his family. Family dinners, in her opinion, were rarely comfortable affairs. But that wouldn't help her get Affairs by Amanda on a firmer financial foundation.

"Ahem. What time are your parents expecting us?"

"Soon. I'll save the tour of the third-floor gym, sauna and steam shower and the basement for later. As much as I'd prefer to keep you here—" he dipped his head to indicate the bed "—we need to go."

She appreciated his restraint because apparently she'd lost hers—and her perspective right along with it. This weekend was all about business. And that meant meeting his well-connected parents was high on her to-do list.

Like it or not.

If Alex's home had been impressive, Amanda found his parents' French Chateau–styled waterfront mansion in Old Greenwich downright intimidating even in the dark. Well-placed landscape uplighting illuminated the sheer scale of the place.

Her stomach felt as if she'd swallowed a witch's bubbling cauldron of some hot brew. Why was she nervous about meeting his parents? They were merely prospective clients, not prospective in-laws, and she'd grown up in affluent circles.

It was because of the job, the connections and the possibility of tapping into Greenwich society's deep pockets for future events. The results of this meeting could make Affairs by Amanda financially secure.

But she'd interviewed for jobs with society's movers and shakers before, and those hadn't made her this nervous. And thanks to her family and her Vassar education, she knew many über-wealthy people. But still, the unexplainable butterflies tormented her.

The front door of the house opened and a tall, lanky, dark-haired teen came out. Despite the frosty temperature he wasn't wearing a coat over his short-sleeved Giants T-shirt. Unsmiling, he strolled toward the car as they climbed out.

"He looks just like you," she told Alex, when he joined her at the end of the long walkway.

Alex's eyes narrowed and his face seemed to tense. Why?

"I take it that's your brother?"

"That's Zack."

She noted and disregarded the odd note in Alex's voice. Bringing a woman home to meet the folks implied things they didn't want implied. Was he as uncomfortable about this as she? "He's cute. As I imagine you were at seventeen. I'm sure you were a lady-killer in training."

He shot her an odd look but said nothing, since Zack had reached them. Alex held out his upraised hand, grasped palms with his brother in a boys-from-the-hood kind of handshake and then the males slapped each other's back in an almost-hug. Zack, obviously playing it cool, didn't crack a smile, but his excitement over seeing Alex sparkled in eyes the same brown shot with gold as Alex's.

"Amanda, this is Zack. Zack, my *friend* Amanda Crawford."

She shot Alex a quick questioning glance. What was that about? The emphasis he'd put on the word *friend* implied they were more than friendly, and she didn't want to give his family the wrong impression. Sure, they were lovers at the moment, but that would soon change. This was merely business with benefits.

Amanda offered her hand. "It's nice to meet you, Zack."

The teen surveyed her from head to toe. Did she detect a tinge of resentment in his eyes? He briefly shook hands. "You, too."

Zack turned his attention back to Alex. "The 'rents are waiting inside."

Alex placed a hand in the small of her back and guided her up the walk and into the house. The foyer was as opulent as the outside of the house had led her to expect. The decor emitted an old-money feel with an intricately patterned hardwood floor, classic antique furniture, luxurious Persian carpets and artwork by Albert Bierstadt and Frederic Church on the soaring wainscoted walls.

Her stomach twisted tighter with each echoing step as she and Alex followed Zack's loping stride into a paneled den. A man and woman rose with welcoming smiles on their faces from the sofas that flanked the brick fireplace. It was easy to see that Alex and Zack had inherited their mother's coloring and patrician bone structure. The blue-eyed blond man was the exact opposite coloring-wise of the woman by his side.

"Mom, Dad, this is Amanda Crawford. Amanda, my parents, Ellen and Harry Harper."

Alex's mother immediately stepped forward and pulled Amanda into an exuberant hug. The warmth of her greeting took Amanda aback. And then Ellen put her at arm's length, clasped both of Amanda's hands and beamed as if she'd just been voted Time's Woman of the Year. "We are so glad Alex has finally brought someone home."

Apprehension tickled Amanda's toes.

"Mother, I told you this wasn't—"

"Oh, hush, Alex. Go pour us drinks, darling. I can't wait to get to know your Amanda better."

Amanda's uneasiness multiplied. She gave Alex a fix-this glare. He shrugged and she wanted to smack him. Instead she forced a smile and turned back to her hostess when Alex surprisingly complied with his mother's command.

"Thank you for inviting me to dinner, Mrs. Harper."

"Ellen. We don't stand on formality here. And we're happy to have you."

As soon as Ellen released her, Alex's father took her place and captured Amanda's hand in both of his. "It's nice to finally meet you, Amanda. Your father and I have known each other for years. He's spoken of you often. When I talked with Theo this afternoon I told him you were coming home with Alex tonight. We couldn't be more pleased."

Amanda barely stifled a groan. The evening couldn't get worse. Alex's parents and hers thought there was more to this relationship than party planning and stellar, though temporary sex. When it was over, she'd have to listen to her parents' lectures about yet another failed relationship.

Oh, joy. She couldn't wait for that.

Five

Amanda Crawford was a professional charmer. The past two days had only reinforced Alex's opinion that she was the woman for the job of increasing his visibility and connections. No other woman would do.

His family's overexuberant welcome Friday night had thrown her, but after one panicked glance at him, she'd sailed in like a trouper and worked her magic for the remainder of the weekend, putting everyone at ease and keeping the conversation flowing. She'd even teased Zack out of his surly mood—a mood Zack seemed to exhibit more often than not these days.

Amanda was smoother than the Rémy Martin Louis XIII cognac he brought out to celebrate special occasions. It was only because Alex knew her agenda that he'd recognized the subtle, skillful questioning she'd employed to tease Zack's hobbies and interests from him this weekend.

Pulling out his BlackBerry, Alex made a note to schedule some one-on-one time with Zack to get to the bottom of the bad attitude. It frustrated him that he could give only brotherly advice. Eighteen years ago he'd wanted nothing to do with fatherhood and would have readily paid for an abortion. And that would have been a mistake. Now he wanted to claim his son, to tell Zack how proud he was of him. But that could never happen.

Shoving away the nagging thoughts, he put his Black-Berry away and studied Amanda's profile as the taxi neared her apartment building. She had her face turned toward the window, apparently enthralled by the gently falling snow or the bustle of pedestrians. More likely ignoring him.

Except for Amanda Crawford, women didn't ignore him.

He could feel her putting distance between them. In fact, he had felt the chill since they'd boarded the train to Grand Central Terminal. She'd wanted him to stay in Greenwich, let her travel home alone. But he always saw his women to the door.

The only downside to the weekend was when they'd said good-bye three hours ago, after Sunday brunch. His mother had been wearing a smug smile that told him she was already planning a wedding. His and Amanda's.

That wasn't going to happen, but she refused to believe him no matter how many times he'd told her he spent too much time dealing with the financial fallout caused by nasty divorces to be interested in signing up for that headache. It concerned him that his mother had bonded so quickly with Amanda. But that was partially his fault. He'd never taken a woman home before.

The taxi pulled to a stop at 721 Park Avenue. Alex climbed from the car and turned to hand Amanda out of the vehicle. The sight of her long legs beneath a short cashmere dress hit him, along with memories of her kneeling above him in bed, wrapped around him in the shower and stretched out on the rug in front of his fireplace. His heart kicked into overdrive.

He stepped to the back of the car, paid the driver and took Amanda's suitcase from the cabbie before she could reach it.

"Alex, there's no need to walk me up. Take the taxi back to the station."

"We need to discuss Zack's party. I want to know what you and my mother cooked up when she banished the men of the house to play billiards."

Amanda hugged her coat tighter around her middle. Snowflakes settled on her fuzzy pink knit hat. "Nothing earth-shattering, but she and Zack gave me some ideas to work with. We have plenty of time to plan his birthday. Your company party is a different story. You change the subject every time I bring that up."

"Correction—I've put the event in your capable hands and I trust you with the details."

"I know you said you wanted me to handle everything, but I'd really like your input on a few items. Carte blanche sounds like a good idea to an event planner, but I've learned the hard way those kinds of events rarely live up to the expectations of the one who's footing the bill. You have expectations whether you realize it or not."

Since he wasn't ready to say good-night, he'd play along. "We'll grab a couple of coffees and your favorite chocolate muffins, and you can tell me what else you've come up with."

Talking wasn't all he intended to do. The minute she

finished her muffin he'd untie the knot at the waist of her plum colored dress and unwrap her, one pale, delicious inch at a time. If he could wait that long.

His hunger for her these past three months had bordered on an obsession. Why hadn't having her—repeatedly—lessened his need? It was a weakness he wouldn't tolerate, and that meant getting past it.

Amanda's less-than-enthusiastic expression would give a less confident man performance anxiety. But he knew he pleased her in bed. She wasn't shy about expressing her pleasure or asking for what she needed. And that turned him on like nothing else.

"It's been a long weekend, Alex. I need to prepare for the upcoming week and—"

"Invite me up, Amanda."

Her lips parted at his gruff tone. She held his gaze. He could tell she was considering refusing. He stepped closer, invading her space, and nudged his thigh against hers, earning a gratifying hitch of her breath.

"Fine. You can come up for a few minutes."

They made a quick, silent detour to Park Café and then returned to her building. The doorman watched them from the moment they entered, his narrowed gaze falling on Amanda's suitcase in Alex's hand.

"Hello, Henry," Amanda greeted him.

The doorman nodded. "Good afternoon, Ms. Crawford, Mr. Harper."

Alex nodded a greeting and escorted Amanda across the white marble-floored lobby and around the doorman's desk. He had learned to trust his first impressions of people and there was something about the man's eyes and body language that bothered him.

Amanda looked up at Alex as they crossed the lobby. "I cannot get over how much your brother looks like you. It's almost as if he's a carbon copy. He has your coloring, your gestures and even a similar speech pattern."

The back of Alex's neck prickled. She had spent a lot of time with Zack. Had she guessed the truth? "We're brothers. Siblings have similarities."

"Since I don't have any brothers or sisters I wouldn't know. You both look exactly like your mother. I couldn't find any trace of your father in either you or Zack."

He didn't want to pursue this conversation. He hit the elevator call button since her hands were full with the coffee and muffin bag and her oversize tote bag.

"Did I tell you how much I enjoyed having you in my bed all weekend?" He leaned toward her and pitched his voice low so Henry couldn't overhear.

Her breath caught and desire expanded her pupils, igniting a burn in his gut. She darted a quick glance over his shoulder toward the doorman's desk and then hit him with a small naughty smile that knocked the air from his lungs. "You might have mentioned it. Once or twice."

Hunger pulsed through him. "I want to stay tonight, Amanda."

Her cheeks flushed. The elevator doors opened. She hustled into the car, pivoted on her spike-heeled ankle boots and faced him as the doors closed. "You have to stop doing that. We're temporary, remember?"

He stroked her jaw with a fingertip and then bent to sip from her lips once, twice, a third time. It wasn't enough. Not nearly enough. He drew back until only the tips of their noses touched.

"Stop telling you I want you? Or stop spending the

night? I'm not moving in, Amanda. I want to be lost in you again. We're good together."

Her head tipped back to rest against the wall. Staring up at him, she swallowed, licked her lips and inhaled a shuddery breath.

"You can stay tonight. But, Alex, when your party ends, we end. Okay? I'm not looking for forever. And neither are you. Let's not try to make something out of this temporary diversion that it's not. Your parents already think… Well, you're going to have to convince them that it's not going to happen."

Interesting to be on the receiving end of that comment for a change. Interesting. But not enjoyable. "No. It's not. I don't do marriage."

He wanted her for more than a few weeks, but he'd worry about changing her mind later. At the most they'd last a few months. He'd never met a woman he wanted to spend the rest of his life with. Not even Zack's mother. Especially not Zack's mother. Chelsea Brooks was one devious, deceitful, greedy bitch. Too bad he hadn't known that before their affair.

But Amanda wasn't like Chelsea in any way. He leaned as close as the carrier of coffee Amanda held between them would allow and lowered his head. She met him halfway. Her lips parted and her tongue met his. Silky, slick, seductive. Need rose within him. He angled his head to deepen the kiss. Her scent filled his nose. Releasing her suitcase, he burrowed his hands beneath her heavy coat to the warmth of her waist and dug his fingers into the soft cashmere of her dress. His palms wicked up her heat, spreading it up his arms and through his torso.

A few months of this would be enough.

It would have to be. But at the moment his hunger for her seemed insatiable.

A chime announced they'd reached Amanda's floor. He lifted his head and inhaled a sobering breath a second before the doors glided open. The interruption was a good thing, since he wasn't into public displays of affection.

How did she do that to him? Make him forget where he was and that the elevator probably had security cameras? In his business, image was everything. He couldn't afford to be caught with his pants down—literally *or* metaphorically. But then again, no one at 721 Park cared what he did. He wasn't a resident. And in Greenwich he kept a low profile. The press ignored him to focus on the celebrities who made their home within the town's borders.

He released Amanda, grabbed the handle of her suitcase and followed her out. He had to admit he found the slightly dazed look in her grey eyes gratifying. Nice to know he wasn't the only one in a hormonal fog.

But like the weather, this fog would eventually lift.

Why had she let Alex talk her into this? Amanda asked herself as she unlocked her apartment door.

Because he gave you that look—the one that deep-sixes your ability to think. A look he's probably been perfecting since he was younger than Zack.

And he bribed you with a muffin.

God, you're easy.

After sixty almost uninterrupted hours of Alex's company, she needed to get away from the man. Watching him interact with Zack, she'd seen a side of him this weekend that she could have lived without—a caring, gentle, understanding side that had gone a long way toward eroding Alex's player image. And she couldn't afford to see him as anything less than a player. Alex was all about temporary and so was she. She liked it that way.

She shouldered open her door and marched straight into her kitchen, where she deposited her tote, the coffee and the bakery bag on the table. Alex followed.

"Have a seat. I'll get your file. It's in my office."

He caught her elbow as she passed. "Eat first. I know you like your muffins hot and fresh from the oven."

"That's because the chocolate chips will still be gooey and delicious." Thinking about it made her mouth water. She shrugged out of her coat. He took it from her and laid hers and his over the back of the extra chair.

Get it over with. Feed him. Update him. Get rid of him.

While she grabbed plates from the cabinet he tore open the bag. The scent of chocolate and roasted walnuts filled the room. Her stomach growled as she climbed onto one of the high stools. Alex did the same beside her. Their knees bumped beneath the table, sending a spray of sparks northward.

Good grief. She'd exhausted a year's quota of orgasms this weekend. How could she still get all shivery and hot from just bumping knees with the man?

Doing her best to ignore him in his charcoal cashmere V-neck sweater and snug black jeans, she peeled away the muffin's paper. Melted chocolate quickly coated her fingers. If she were alone she'd lick her fingers. But with Alex here she had to act like less of a glutton.

She rose to find some napkins, but Alex caught her wrist, pulling her between his splayed knees. His desire-filled gaze locked with hers as he lifted her hand to his mouth and laved her fingertip with a slick swipe. She shivered with want. He moved on to the next messy fingertip and the next.

Her eyelids grew heavy and drifted closed. Not good. Lack of sight only accentuated her other senses. She lost herself in his scent, the brackets of his strong thighs around her hips, the hot caress of his tongue swirling around each fingertip and the feel of his hand on the thin skin of her wrist. He couldn't possibly miss her racing pulse beneath his thumb.

She forced her eyes open. He finished the left hand and moved to her right. Desire flushed his cheekbones with dark color, making her feel hotter and gooier than the muffin's melted chips.

But she didn't protest because she couldn't find her voice. He dipped his finger into a glistening melted chocolate spot in his muffin and then painted her lips with a slow sweep. The intense concentration of his dark eyes on her mouth made breathing nearly impossible. He bent his head and licked and nibbled off the chocolate.

She nearly collapsed into a puddle at his feet.

Stop him. Stop this. Wanting him this much can't be good.

The warm, wet, slow pass of his tongue dragged a moan from her. He took advantage of her parted lips to deepen the kiss. She savored the delicious combination of chocolate and Alex. But then he drew back. Relieved to escape the onslaught—and yes, a little disappointed, too—she stared at him.

A slow smile worked its way across his lips. He pinched off a morsel of muffin and brought it to her lips. "Open."

She dumbly complied. The rich, chocolaty taste filled her mouth. Her taste buds did their usual dance. But she would rather be tasting the man tormenting her. She swallowed. As if he'd read her mind, his mouth covered hers again. He devoured her mouth with sips, nips and swirls. Her thoughts whirled like fruit in a blender. He had her off balance mentally and physically.

A tug at her waist sobered her. She jerked back. "What are you doing?"

"Wait and see." He pulled again at the tie of her wraparound dress. Cool air swept her torso as he brushed the fabric aside.

Her still-sticky fingers kept her from grabbing her dress as it slid off her shoulders and caught at her elbows. She'd never get chocolate stains out. "We're supposed to be going over your part—"

He smeared a streak of chocolate just above the lace of her bra, dipping into her cleavage.

"Hey!" And then he bent to lap it up. Her protest turned into a groan. "Working, Alex. We're supposed to be *working*."

But the heat inside her intensified, liquefying her knees. Her legs weakened. She grasped the table's edge to keep herself upright. He painted another melted chocolate chip stripe on her other breast, then laved her clean. His fingers hooked her bra straps and lowered them to her upper arms, baring her nipples, which he circled with more chocolate paint. The heat of his moist mouth enclosed her, the suction tugging at the desire deep in her belly and pulling forth a response she thought he'd exhausted.

She bit her lip on a whimper of want. She would never be able to eat her favorite food again without remembering this.

"Touch me," he ordered against her breast.

"Hands. Chocolate. Cashmere." She couldn't retrieve more from the mush he'd made of her brain.

Alex stood, ripped his sweater and the T-shirt he'd worn beneath it over his head and tossed them.

Food sex. A new one for her. New and exciting. But then sex with Alex had been an adventure each time. One she'd have to end. Soon.

She crumbled off a corner of the moist cake and swiped her finger through a melted morsel. Debating her options, she decided to plant a fingerprint on each flat nipple. Holding his gaze, she bent to lick him clean.

His pupils expanded and his hands fastened on her waist, tightening and releasing as she worked zealously to cleanse his skin. He groaned. "Watching you eat your muffins has been driving me crazy for months."

Stunned, she straightened. "Watching me eat turns you on?"

"It's the sensual way you savor each bite. I knew you'd wear the same expression when I was inside you."

Heat rushed through her, and her pulse quickened to double time. "I do?"

"Yes. Drop the dress." His low voice rumbled over her skin like the roar of an approaching motorcycle.

She had to be out of her mind to comply. They were here to work. But work would have to wait. She dropped her arms by her side and let the dress go. The soft fabric drifted down, caressing her calves as it passed to puddle around her ankle boots.

Alex unfastened her bra and sent it on the same path, leaving her in nothing but her lavender lace thong and shoes. He devoured her with his gaze, lingering over her breasts, slowly sweeping her belly, her hips and her thighs before taking an equally meandering return trip.

His hands bracketed her waist and stroked a swath of heat, first upward to tease the undersides of her breasts and then downward, dragging the thong to her knees as he passed. He bent to press an openmouthed kiss over the tattoo on her left hip, stealing her breath, and then he lifted her onto the stool she'd abandoned and whisked her lingerie over her ankles. He splayed his hands on her knees, separated them and stepped between her thighs. His arms banded around her, bringing them chest to scorching chest as his mouth branded hers in a hot, wet, carnal kiss. His tongue plunged deep.

His hands swept her back, her waist and finally her breasts. He stroked and tweaked her nipples until hunger consumed her and she squirmed with need. His hands traveled lower, finding her wetness and igniting a fire no amount of moisture could put out. Alex had great hands, she'd grant him that. And a great mouth. And a great—

The nip of his teeth on her neck cut off her thoughts. She arched into his touch, relishing each stroke of his fingers until she teetered on the edge of release and she would need more than just his hand.

He had on too many clothes. The supple skin of his back goose-bumped beneath the light rake of her nails. His buttocks clenched under her caress. She dragged her fingers around the inside of his belt, opened the buckle and lowered his zipper. Impatient to pleasure him as he was her, she shoved his pants and briefs over his hips and curled her fingers around his erection. His hot, silky flesh thickened and pulsed with the stroke of her hand.

Alex broke the kiss on a hissed inhalation and

withdrew a condom from his pocket before letting his pants fall to the floor.

Striving for mental distance, she nodded to the packet in his hand. "You keep those on you at all times, huh?"

"When I'm with you, yes. Otherwise, no. I'm too old to think like a kid who's always prepared on the off chance he might get lucky."

Not what she wanted to hear. That made him sound as if he weren't a player. She reminded herself they had only thirteen days left. Less than two weeks to gorge herself on Alex's talent in bed, the shower, the hot tub, or in the kitchen, as the case may be tonight. And then she would quit him cold turkey. Part of her wanted to store up as much sexual satisfaction as she could until then. Another part warned her to pull back now before she became as addicted to this man as she was to Park Café's chocolate muffins.

Her needy, demanding side won the argument. She curled her fingers around his nape, threaded them through his hair and pulled him forward for another kiss. Alex didn't hesitate to step up to the plate. You had to like a man who was confident enough not to be threatened when a woman turned aggressive.

He let her set the tone for the kiss. Or maybe he was just as desperate and edgy and needy as she was. Their teeth clashed. Their noses bumped. But his soft lips, slick tongue and dexterous hands kept her fire stoked.

One corner of her mind heard the condom wrapper tear. A tiny part realized he was taking care of protection, but her pulse roared when he grasped her hips, dug his fingers into her bottom, and pulled her to the edge of the high stool.

He nudged her entrance, slicking his tip in her moisture, and then he thrust forward. She tore her mouth from his to gasp as he filled her. When he withdrew, she dug her nails into his buttocks and pulled him back. He slid deep again and withdrew over and over. His teeth nipped her neck, making her gasp as a shock of longing bolted through her. She tilted her head to grant him better access.

Her pleasure built, fueled by his thumb circling her center. She wound her legs around his hips, savored the steam of his breath on her neck, her jaw, her cheek. And then orgasm reverberated through her like blasts from a bass speaker, making her body pulse and contract.

Alex's hands tightened on her bottom, his tempo increased and his mouth covered hers in a desperate, edgy kiss. His groan filled her mouth as he stiffened with his own release.

Every cell in her body felt alive and aware of this man and of this moment. Why hadn't any other man ever felt this good or made her feel this good?

It wasn't fair that she'd finally found one who rocked her world. And she couldn't keep him. He was too much a part of that restrictive world she'd grown up in.

The one in which she'd never fit.

Six

A cell phone jarred Amanda from sleep. She rolled over and blindly, groggily slapped around the nightstand until her fingers closed around the device. She fumbled it open.

"Hello." Cracking an eyelid, she looked at her digital clock. Five-thirty. Who would be calling at this ungodly hour on a Monday morning?

"Amanda, darling." Her mother's voice shattered what was left of her sleepy haze. "I am so proud of you."

Not words she'd heard from a parental unit before. Was she dreaming? A warm glow suffused her...until she started wondering what she'd done to earn that rare proclamation. Nothing came to mind.

A strong arm banded her waist, pulling her back under the covers. Heat blanketed her back. Teeth nipped her shoulder, awakening her in an entirely different way.

Alex. He'd stayed the night. Again. She'd worry about

that later. But now she couldn't stop herself from leaning back into him and savoring his embrace and the morning arousal pressed against her buttocks.

She forced her attention back to her caller. "Good morning, Mother. What are you talking about?"

The hand skating from her waist to her breast distracted her, but felt too good to stop him. Alex knew exactly how and where to touch her to reap the maximum benefit. The kink factor of enjoying having Alex naked against her when her mother was yapping in her ear was off the charts.

"I'm talking about your association with Alexander Harper. I'm so glad to see you finally coming to your senses."

The words snuffed out the kindling glow. Amanda sat up, dislodging Alex's arm and lips. A chill that had nothing to do with the blankets falling away from her bare skin rushed over her.

"My friend at the paper says you spent the weekend with the Harper family."

This was not good. Not good at all. Her parents would expect more than a fling, and she couldn't deliver anything more than another disappointment. She glanced at Alex and found his questioning dark eyes trained on her. "What friend? What paper?"

"She writes for the Greenwich society column. They're running a story on the weekend's happenings, and apparently you and your beau were seen all about town."

Her beau? "It's not what you think. Alex and I were looking for a location for his brother's birthday party. And don't tell anybody that because it's supposed to be a surprise party."

"You can concoct whatever tale you wish, dear, but my friend says you and Alexander were quite friendly in the photos they snapped."

Amanda cringed at the emphasis. Yes, she and Alex had held hands and, yes, they'd sneaked in a few heated embraces and kisses during the walk around town. How could she help it? He was too sexy. But she would have kept her hands and lips to herself if she'd known someone was spying and that the news would get back to her parents.

Mental memo: No more PDAs.

"Amanda, your father and I approve wholeheartedly. A man like Alexander would be such an asset. He's exactly what you need, and he makes enough that you'd be able to give up that business of yours."

Amanda gritted her teeth to hold back a groan at the jab at Affairs by Amanda. As often as she heard the barbs, they should bounce right off by now, but they still hurt like someone ripping off a scab. "Mother, you're not willing to give up your business. Why should I be willing to give up mine?"

"Because mine makes scads of money and it's respe—"

"Respectable. Yes. I know." Why did she bother to rehash this argument over and over? She would never win.

But she wanted to. That's why she kept trying.

Alex caught her attention as he rose from her bed, all lean, long, muscular and naked. His golden skin, lightly dusted with dark whorls of hair, mesmerized her. Her gaze fell to his erection. Desire licked her insides, shocking her since she still had her mother yapping in her ear.

How twisted was it to want to reach out and touch someone intimately with your mother on the phone?

"Amanda!"

Oops. What had she missed? "I'm sorry, Mom, what did you say?"

"I said you need to bring him home for dinner."

Amanda's stomach turned. "I don't think that's a good idea."

"He comes from a good family."

"Yes, I know. But—"

"He owns a house and a successful law firm. I don't think your previous disasters owned more than their clothes."

Ouch. But in most cases true.

"You have to grow up sometime and quit this party nonsense. You could do worse than Alexander Harper. In fact, you have. Often."

Another scab ripped off leaving her raw and bleeding. She couldn't handle this kind of abuse without caffeine. "Mom, I have to get ready for work now. I'll call you back when I have time to chat."

No, she wouldn't.

"Get me a list of dates when Alexander can visit, and your father and I will check our calendars." Her mother disconnected, leaving Amanda in a funk she knew would ruin the rest of her day. Talking with her parents always did.

"Problem?" Alex asked, as he returned from the bathroom.

"Nothing I can't handle." She threw off the sheet and rose.

He snagged her around the waist and pulled her close, molding his naked frame to hers. One big palm cupped her bottom and kneaded. "Join me in the shower."

"Alex—" Desire hit her hard and fast, followed by a crazy chaser of an idea.

What if she kept Alex around? Not forever, but for a

while. Just until she got Affairs by Amanda on a firmer footing. Her parents might get off her back.

There would be hell to pay when the relationship ended....

But wouldn't it be worth it to have her parents' approval for as long as it lasted?

She studied his face and weighed the risks. "Apparently news of our relationship is about to hit the Greenwich papers. Perhaps we should consider extending our affair until after Zack's party. It will make the planning easier to keep secret."

His eyes narrowed. She waited for him to voice the questions she could see forming.

"Works for me," he said instead.

She hoped she didn't live to regret extending her temporary affair.

Deposit one million dollars in the Grand Cayman account listed below or the truth about your "brother's" true parentage will be made public.

Do not go to the police or you will regret it.

Tension invaded Alex's muscles and a chill enveloped him Wednesday afternoon as he read the single sheet of boldfaced type.

Who'd sent this?

He scanned the letter again, but it yielded nothing more than the demand and banking information. His name and office address had been typed. There was no return address on the letter or the envelope and no identifiable handwriting.

The red-stamped *Confidential* inscription on the left

side of the envelope didn't trip any triggers. He received mail marked this way on a daily basis. It was the nature of his business. Usually there was nothing personal in the contents, but Moira had decided long ago to pass those letters on to him unopened. He returned them to her as soon as he discovered they fell under her jurisdiction.

Which led him back to who could have done this. Less than a handful of people knew the truth about Zack's parentage. He and Chelsea. His parents. The attorney who'd handled Zack's adoption. But his parents wouldn't do this, and the attorney was too straitlaced and respectable. That left Chelsea.

Was Zack's birth mother up to her old tricks? She'd sold Zack once already. In the past eighteen years she'd shown no desire whatsoever to get to know their son or even to meet him. And she had spending issues. The woman burned through money like a California wildfire rips through the canyons during a drought.

Chelsea was greedy. She'd come to him for money several times since their split. But he'd never believed her to be stupid. She'd have to know she'd be the first he'd suspect. He dropped the letter on his desk, picked up the phone and punched out her number.

"What the hell are you trying to do?" he asked, as soon as she answered.

"Alex? What are you talking about?"

"The extortion letter."

"What?"

"Did you write a letter threatening to expose Zack's parentage?"

"No! I— No. I wouldn't do that." Her shock sounded genuine.

"It wouldn't be the first time you tried to squeeze money out of my family. Nor the second. Or even the thir—"

"Alex, I didn't. I swear it. The gallery is doing well now. You should stop by and see it. We could do dinner afterward."

The suggestive lilt of her voice did nothing for him. She'd tried to trap him into marriage almost nineteen years ago, and she'd periodically made a play for him every few years when she was between men. But he wasn't interested in opportunistic women who put a price tag on their children.

Usually he ignored her advances because reacting in any way seemed to encourage her. "I'm not interested, Chelsea. In your gallery or anything else you're offering."

"Not even if I offer you an amazing opportunity to invest in a fabulous new artist?"

Was that what she was calling her need for money these days? "No, thanks. Who have you told about Zack?"

"No one. I promise. That's not a part of my life I care to share."

That he believed. He ended the call.

If it wasn't Chelsea or one of her cronies, then who could it be? Alex stood and paced to the windows. Apprehension twanged his nerves like guitar strings. He had to protect Zack. No matter what the cost. Otherwise, this would hurt his "brother" and possibly push Zack from surly to outright rebellious.

What should he do?

Pay the money? No. Crooks always came back for more. Then what? Ignore it? Call the police?

The only permanent solution was to eliminate the threat. That meant going to the police no matter what the note said. But he couldn't trust just anybody with something this volatile.

So who could he trust?

A private investigator might work, but that could take too much time.

The detective who'd interviewed him twice after Marie Endicott's murder at 721 Park seemed like a straight-up guy. Perhaps Arnold McGray could recommend someone within the department who could discreetly handle this case.

Alex dug in his wallet for the detective's card, but before he could reach for the phone his intercom buzzed.

He didn't have time for interruptions now. "Yes?"

"Amanda Crawford is here for your lunch appointment."

Amanda. The current crisis had knocked her pending arrival out of his head—a first since thoughts of her had taken up residence in his brain several months ago. His interest in her should be waning by now, but the leap of his pulse said otherwise.

Because you've yet to utilize her to further your career.

Right.

Could Amanda be behind this? Since the weekend in Greenwich she'd remarked more than once on the similarities between him and Zack.

"Alex? Should I send her in?" Moira's voice interrupted his thoughts.

"Yes." Amanda didn't seem the type to stoop to extortion or bribery. But she was short of cash and she'd just spent the weekend with his family. Had she guessed Zack's parentage? He didn't know how that was possible, but that could be why she'd suddenly agreed to extend their affair when she'd been adamant only a few days ago about ending it.

His office door opened. Moira ushered Amanda in. He searched Amanda's face for a sign that she'd sent the extortion note or that she knew who had. But her grey gaze met his directly and her smile looked sincere. A slight flush pinked her cheeks. Nothing about her slender body wrapped in a fuzzy powder-blue sweater and a short suede skirt looked evasive or expectant. She carried her ever-present briefcase and wore the requisite ankle-breaking heels—this time in the same suede as her skirt.

If not her, what about her crooked ex? Had Amanda shared her suspicions with Curtis Wilks?

"I'll bring lunch in when it arrives," Moira said, before backing out and closing the door.

Amanda took two steps into the room and then stopped. Wearing a puzzled expression, she searched his face. "Is something wrong?"

He wasn't about to tell her. "No."

She shrugged, crossed the room and swung her briefcase onto the desktop. The movement sent the extortion note flying. With rapid reflexes, she bent over the desk and slapped a hand over the fluttering page to keep it from falling to the floor. The move made her short skirt rise up and gave him an arousing glance at the back of her lean thighs.

"Caught it." She slowly straightened with the sheet in her hand. Before he could snatch it from her, her gaze fell to the letter. Her eyes widened as she read the large font and then she lifted her gaze to his. Her shock appeared authentic, but there was a trace of something else in her eyes— something missing from her expression—that made his gut clench. Amanda displayed a total lack of surprise.

"Alex, what are you going to do?"

"That's none of your business."

She stiffened. "I'm not trying to pry. But you have to do something. This would hurt Zack if he doesn't already know."

Apprehension chilled him. He struggled to keep his churning emotions from showing. "If he doesn't know what?"

She bit her bottom lip and her expression turned cagey. "That he's not your father's son."

How had she found out? And what would she do with the information? "Why would you think that?"

"Besides the almost-eighteen-year age difference between the two of you?"

"Yes."

"While you men were doing guy things, your mother mentioned something in passing about how much she re-gretted missing your high school graduation but that she couldn't be there because she'd been living in Paris when Zack was born. She seemed to regret the slip, so I didn't pursue the topic. But after reading this… It seems to confirm what I thought."

"And what did you think?"

"That maybe your parents had separated for a while and that your mother might have had an affair during their time apart. That's nothing to be ashamed of. A lot of couples have trial separations."

His mother had lived in Paris with Chelsea during the pregnancy. Was Amanda telling the truth and merely curious or was she fishing for details? With so much at stake he couldn't afford to take chances.

"You guessed incorrectly."

"Okay." She sounded unconvinced. She nodded to the letter. "Then what does this mean?"

He took the letter from her. "Don't meddle. This doesn't concern you."

"Well, *excuse* me for caring. What will you do? To protect Zack, I mean."

"I'll handle it."

"I like your brother, Alex, and it's obvious your father adores him. Will Harry help you?"

"Help me what?"

"Come up with the money."

The back of his neck prickled. "You expect me to pay this?"

"What choice do you have? It says don't go to the police."

He weighed her words, her expression and her body language. Was she hiding knowledge of the perpetrator? Did she know more than she was letting on? If she was, he couldn't see it.

"Did you send the note?"

She flinched and then paled. Dark red spots filled her cheeks. "You think I would bribe you? Or hurt Zack?"

She held up a hand before he could reply. "Don't answer that. The fact that you even asked the question says it all. You don't know me. All we have is good sex. And we won't have that for long."

The frost in her voice matched the outside temperature. She opened her briefcase with sharp, decisive movements. "Perhaps we should get to the real reason for my visit. Your party is only ten days away."

"By all means." Because until he got to the bottom of this he couldn't trust her or anyone else.

* * *

Amanda's head was reeling and her heart… Her heart was in serious trouble. She was falling for Alex Harper. Why else would his nasty accusation hurt so badly?

How she'd managed to get through the past hour she would never know. Carefully blanking her expression, she kept her eyes on the number panel above the doors as she took the elevator down from Alex's office after the tense lunch meeting. The darn box stopped on almost every floor, increasing the urgency of her need to escape the high-rise. Her blood pulsed in her ears.

She could not, would not fall for Alex Harper.

Too late?

Maybe.

No. Not too late. She wouldn't let it be too late.

But a sense of doom settled over her. Why did she always fall for the wrong guys? Did she have a masochistic streak? Did she like pain and suffering and relationship train wrecks?

Apparently so. She certainly drew disastrous romances like Times Square does New Year's Eve revelers.

How could Alex sleep with her, loan her money, hire her and introduce her to his family if he distrusted her so much? She'd barely hung on to her professional demeanor during the past hour as that question had tumbled around in her brain.

The elevator finally reached the ground floor. Amanda spilled out of the cubicle and into the lobby with the rest of the crowd. She numbly followed them through the revolving glass doors, onto the sidewalk and straight into a cold wind that cut so deeply she tugged her coat tighter.

Undecided which way to turn, she paused on the

concrete. Should she go home to wallow in her discovery alone or somewhere else? She needed a chocolate chocolate chip muffin and a latte. Or a raspberry martini. Definitely a martini. Maybe two.

Lovely. The man's driving you to drink in the middle of the day.

Would Julie be up for an afternoon of hooky? Amanda pulled her cell phone from her pocket and headed toward her apartment, but then remembered Julie was pregnant. Her former roomie wouldn't drink alcohol. And drinking alone wasn't a habit Amanda wanted or needed to acquire. She shoved her phone back into her pocket.

"Amanda!" a deep voice called from behind her—a voice she didn't want to hear at the moment. She quickened her stride.

"Amanda, wait."

An uncooperative crosswalk light and a steady stream of taxis trapped her between escape and Alex.

She knew the instant he stopped behind her, even before he gripped her elbow and pulled her out of the flow of pedestrians who surged forward now that the light had changed—five seconds too late.

Alex swung her around to face him. "I'm sorry."

The apology surprised her. She hadn't taken Alex for the apologizing type. And then she noticed he'd come after her without his coat. He had to be freezing. She was cold even with her coat, scarf and hat.

"I'm worried about how Zack will take this and how badly he'll be hurt. I don't know how to protect him. I shouldn't have accused you. But I have no idea where this threat is coming from or how to deal with it."

Hmm. A man who admitted uncertainty. Interesting.

And rare. The men of her past had always bluffed their way through any ignorance—even though it usually came back to bite them.

Alex's obvious love and concern for his brother eased some of her pain. "What 'this' do you mean? That Zack is not his father's natural son? Yes, that will upset him initially, but your father accepted Zack, loves him and raised him as his own. Zack will get over the hurt when he remembers that your father was there for him when it counted."

"I never said Zack wasn't my father's."

"You didn't have to. He's clearly your mother's child."

If anything, Alex's face tensed even more, and the cold wind painted ruddy stripes on his cheekbones and tossed his overlong hair. He looked like he had something to say, but remained silent and shoved his hands into his suit coat pockets. She fisted hers against the urge to smooth his windblown locks, to tangle her fingers in the strands and pull him close for a kiss that would curl her toes and chase away the chill.

That he'd shut her out after sleeping with her for the past nine days stung. She shifted in her boots. "You should go back inside, Alex. It's too cold to be out here without your overcoat."

He looked ready to argue, but nodded instead. "I'll see you tonight."

She had to pull back while she still could. Letting him spend so many nights at her place was guaranteed to only order up a dose of heartbreak.

"No. I think…I want a little space, Alex."

His eyebrows lowered and he searched her face. "What about the cocktail party Friday night?"

She fought a grimace. She'd forgotten about the

charity affair Alex had asked her to attend with him. Accompanying him to a rich-and-famous-filled event would give her another opportunity for exposure and to make connections—one she couldn't afford to refuse. And she'd promised. She always kept her promises.

"I'll be ready at seven."

But by Friday she'd have her game plan established and her walls firmly back in place. Never again would she make the mistake of forgetting Alex Harper was temporary.

Because today he'd given her a taste of what his eventual dismissal was going to feel like. And she didn't like it.

Seven

"Detective." Alex extended his hand across the paper-stacked desk and shook hands with Arnold McGray.

"Harper." The lean but paunch-bellied, fortysomething detective with salt-and-pepper hair and disillusioned green eyes rose and returned the greeting with a firm grip. "Have a seat and tell me what brings you to my turf."

"I received an extortion note today. I realize extortion is outside of your homicide sphere, but I was hoping you could direct me to someone within the department who could handle this discreetly."

McGray perked up. "Did you bring it with you?"

Alex pulled the clear plastic bag from his coat pocket and passed it across the desk. Before sitting down in a scarred but sturdy wooden chair in front of the desk, he removed his overcoat and draped it over the back of the second chair.

"If your note's related to 721 Park, then it's part of my investigation until I determine otherwise." Without opening the plastic McGray scanned the text, flipped it over and studied the envelope. "What's the secret the perp's threatening to expose?"

Did the detective really need to know?

"Could lead to motive," McGray said, as if reading his doubts.

True. Alex checked over his shoulder to make sure they wouldn't be overheard. "Zack is my son and not my parents'."

"And that's not common knowledge?"

"No."

The detective took a moment to scribble on the pad beside him. "Besides you, who's touched this letter?"

"My assistant, any number of Harper & Associates mailroom employees and Amanda Crawford."

Without moving a hair McGray suddenly seemed more alert. Tension entered his body and his gaze sharpened. If Alex hadn't witnessed the change he would have missed it. "Crawford. Leggy blonde. Lives at 721 Park?"

"Yes."

The detective jotted another line on his pad and then looked up. "And why would she have handled this?"

"She was in my office shortly after I received it."

"Personal relationship or business?"

"Both."

"She have an ax to grind with you?"

"Not that I know of."

"What about with the deceased, Marie Endicott? Anything between the women?"

"I don't believe they knew each other."

"What about Endicott's lover? Crawford know him?"

"Marie had a lover?"

"She was having an affair, and we suspect it was with someone in the building. But Trent Tanford's been ruled out as a suspect, despite the pictures all over the papers preceding Endicott's death of the two of them." He tapped his pen on the desk. "Could Endicott's lover have been someone Crawford was interested in or believed she had prior claim to?"

Alex didn't like the turn of the conversation. The protective surge he felt toward Amanda surprised him. He reined it in. "No. Amanda is relatively new to the building. She was seeing someone else before she moved in. Curtis Wilks."

McGray made a note and then his green eyes narrowed on Alex. "You spend a lot of time at 721. Were you seeing Endicott?"

Alex sat back abruptly, his defenses on full alert. "Are you accusing me of something?"

McGray wiped a hand over his face. "No. And there's no need to start sounding like a lawyer. I'm just asking questions. The damned investigation is going nowhere."

"You've asked me that question before and I told you I have friends at 721. I wasn't involved with Marie Endicott. I've heard she fell or was pushed from the roof. Is that correct?"

"Yes."

"Perhaps you should check the security video."

"The roof video is missing and the visitor log for the night in question is empty. Harper, I don't think your case is related, but it could be. There have been other extortion attempts at 721 recently, so I'm going to hold on

The Silhouette Reader Service — Here's how it works:

Accepting your 2 free books and 2 free mystery gifts places you under no obligation to buy anything. You may keep the books and gifts and return the shipping statement marked "cancel". If you do not cancel, about a month later we'll send you 6 additional books and bill you just $4.05 each in the U.S. or $4.74 each in Canada. That is a savings of at least 15% off the cover price. It's quite a bargain! Shipping and handling is just 25¢ per book, along with any applicable taxes.* You may cancel at any time, but if you choose to continue, every month we'll send you 6 more books, which you may either purchase at the discount price or return to us and cancel your subscription.

*Terms and prices subject to change without notice. Sales tax applicable in N.Y. Canadian residents will be charged applicable provincial taxes and GST. Offer not valid in Quebec. All orders subject to approval. Credit or debit balances in a customer's account(s) may be offset by any other outstanding balance owed by or to the customer. Please allow 4 to 6 weeks for delivery. Offer available while quantities last.

NO POSTAGE
NECESSARY
IF MAILED
IN THE
UNITED STATES

BUSINESS REPLY MAIL

FIRST-CLASS MAIL   PERMIT NO. 717   BUFFALO, NY

POSTAGE WILL BE PAID BY ADDRESSEE

SILHOUETTE READER SERVICE
3010 WALDEN AVE
PO BOX 1867
BUFFALO NY 14240-9952

If offer card is missing write to: Silhouette Reader Service, 3010 Walden Ave., P.O. Box 1867, Buffalo NY 14240-1867

Do You Have the LUCKY KEY?

PLAY THE *Lucky Key Game*

and you can get

FREE BOOKS and FREE GIFTS!

Scratch the gold areas with a coin. Then check below to see the books and gifts you can get!

YES!
I have scratched off the gold areas. Please send me the 2 FREE BOOKS and 2 FREE GIFTS, worth about $10, for which I qualify. I understand I am under no obligation to purchase any books, as explained on the back of this card.

326 SDL EVMH   225 SDL EVQT

FIRST NAME   LAST NAME

ADDRESS

APT.#   CITY

STATE/PROV.   ZIP/POSTAL CODE

www.eHarlequin.com

 2 free books plus 2 free gifts   1 free book

 2 free books   Try Again!

DETACH AND MAIL CARD TODAY!

(S-D-11/08)

© 2008 HARLEQUIN ENTERPRISES LIMITED ® and ™ are trademarks owned and used by the trademark owner and/or its licensee.

to this and let our guys—our *team*—compare the font and paper to the others. Until we've ruled out a connection I'm going to have to assume there is one."

He'd known about Julia being threatened with the exposure of her pregnancy, but he hadn't known about any other incident. Did that put Amanda at risk? He needed to warn her.

"Who else has been threatened?"

McGray rose, clearly ending the interview. "I'm not at liberty to say."

Of course McGray wasn't allowed to discuss an open investigation, but Alex had needed to try. He'd already learned more from the detective today than he'd known previously. Alex stood. "I need a quick response. Can't you check for prints or do a DNA analysis on the saliva on the envelope seal?"

McGray's lips flattened in disgust. "This isn't TV, counselor. You know the real world doesn't solve cases in an hour."

"Right. You're understaffed and overworked, but Zack—"

"You're not dealing with an upstanding citizen here, Harper." He thumped the note with a knuckle. "Don't expect him or her to follow the rules. My advice is to tell your son the truth before someone else does. Kids are resilient. They bounce back. He'll get over it."

"That's not an option." Because unlike what Amanda had said, Zack's birth parents hadn't been there for him. His mother had sold him, and like a damned, dumb kid his real father had taken the easy way out.

And that was a mistake Alex could never forgive himself for making. And after almost eighteen years of deceit Zack would never forgive him. Every bond the two of them had forged would be irreparably shattered.

And Alex refused to go there.

Amanda looked good standing beside Alex at the Metropolitan Club, and she knew it. But knowing they made a striking couple, with him so dark and her so fair and both of them tall, didn't lessen the tension between them—a tension that hadn't been there before he'd received the threatening note two days ago.

Alex's height and the breadth of his custom-tailored tux-clad shoulders made her feel delicate and feminine—something she didn't often experience with her stature and addiction to four-inch heels. But long ago she'd realized all the cute shoes were heels, and she couldn't deny she was tall. So why fight it?

Alex's hand on her waist guaranteed her acceptance into this über-rich fund-raising crowd milling about the grand renaissance revival dining room with its ornate columns and marble-and-gilt-accented decor. Only four hundred of the city's elite had been invited to the ten-thousand-dollars-a-ticket event.

In the past hour Alex had introduced her to several prospective clients and managed to plug Affairs by Amanda numerous times without being too obvious. She gave him points for that. In turn, she'd made a few connections for him that he didn't already have. Her parents were actually good for something—not that they'd ever put in a good word for her business with their friends. If anything, they'd do the contrary. But they had exposed her to a few city bigwigs over the years.

She and Alex made a good team. Not something she

needed to dwell on, though, given the temporary nature of their alliance.

Alex snagged a couple of fresh flutes of champagne from a passing waiter, offered one to her and leaned down. His lips touched her ear and she shivered, almost spilling the golden beverage. The chill between them hadn't nixed his ability to arouse her without effort.

"Have I told you that you look amazing?"

Warmth coursed through her. Warmth she tried to tamp down because come hell or high water she was going to dodge this emotional bullet. And the only way to dodge it was to not get in any deeper with Alex.

"Once or twice. But thank you. It's not something I ever tire of hearing." Nor something she heard very often from her hypercritical parents. She had enough pride to hope the greedy way she sponged up Alex's compliments wasn't pathetically obvious.

Smoothing a hand over her red dress, she scanned the crowd rather than look into Alex's eyes and reveal how much his words had meant to her. She'd bought her designer gown in a secondhand shop. It had still had the tags on it and never been worn. It fit so perfectly it could have been personally designed to drape Amanda's body without alterations. But her mother would be appalled at the idea of Amanda wearing someone else's castoffs.

Dominique Crawford always offered Amanda free clothing—an offer Amanda almost always turned down, because the gesture wasn't made from the goodness of her mother's heart or from any maternal love. No, Dominique wanted to dress her daughter for two reasons. One, for free advertisement of her Dominique Designs, and two, because until she'd heard about Alex she'd thought

Amanda had horrible taste—not just in men—and she wasn't shy about sharing her opinion.

Her mother's frequent phone calls over the past five days attested to her approval of Alex, and Amanda was running out of excuses for not scheduling the requested dinner.

"Showtime," Alex murmured, his breath stirring her hormones along with the hair at her temple. She pasted a smile on her face and turned to see who was approaching. Her parents were cutting a direct line toward them across the marble floor and closing fast. Her good mood evaporated. Her heart thudded with panic. She glanced toward the exit, but her path was packed with well-heeled guests. Too late to make an escape.

Her mother, smiling her best camera-ready smile—faux though it might be—approached with arms extended and issued the requisite air kiss near Amanda's cheeks. "Amanda, darling, you didn't tell me you'd be here tonight."

A deliberate oversight. Otherwise, she'd known her mother would miraculously wrangle a ticket to the sold-out event. But apparently her mother had other sources, because this wasn't one of her usual charities. She had no reason to be here except to snoop on her daughter.

"Hello, Mother. Dad." And because she couldn't avoid introductions, she took a deep breath and prepared to plunge into what promised to be certain disaster.

"May I introduce you to Alex Harper? Alex, my parents, Dominique and Theodore Crawford."

Both were well-known, her mother on an international scale in the fashion industry and her father as a Wall Street CEO.

Alex's grip on her waist tightened. His fingertips slipped beneath the low cut fabric on her back sending awareness skipping up her vertebrae. "It's nice to meet you, Mr. and Mrs. Crawford."

"Dominique, please." She offered a beringed hand which Alex shook once. "Perhaps now we can schedule our dinner. Amanda has been quite difficult about setting a date."

Alex shot Amanda a quick questioning glance. No wonder. She hadn't mentioned her mother's invitation. Another deliberate omission. "Amanda and I have both been busy. Call my office and I'll see what my assistant can do to work you in."

Surprised that he'd backed her, thereby earning even more bonus points, she smiled up at him.

Her mother appeared to handle his evasion well, but when she turned a critical eye on Amanda, Amanda's smile slipped. She braced herself. "Darling, that dress—"

"Doesn't Amanda look amazing?" Alex kissed Amanda's temple and pulled her close to the hard, lean line of his body. His warmth and support seeped into her. "She's easily the most beautiful woman here tonight."

Her mother arched a brow. "I wouldn't say that."

"I would." Firm. Decisive. A don't-argue-with-me tone combined with a drilling stare that probably worked wonders on witnesses in the courtroom. "You have a beautiful, talented and very smart daughter. Congratulations."

Amanda could have kissed him. But that would definitely give her parents the wrong idea.

Surprisingly her mother blinked first. "And what have you two been busy doing besides spending time in Greenwich?"

Not a subtle bone in her mother's body. Dominique always probed, always pried, always pushed.

"Amanda is planning a couple of events for me. She's doing a great job." His knuckle dragged along her spine, making her shiver. Getting turned on in front of her parents was definitely new and uncomfortable territory.

Her mother's eyes narrowed, taking in Alex's protective stance. There would be hell to pay for this little act later. Once Amanda and Alex parted ways her mother would want to know how her daughter had managed to let a good one slip through her fingers.

Dominique turned to her husband. "Did you know the Vandercrofts are here? I must say hello. Nice meeting you, Alex. I look forward to our dinner."

And then she sashayed off with her husband in her wake. Tension drained from Amanda like water being released from a dam.

Alex had gone to bat for her—something none of the guys from her past had ever done. At that moment the ledge slipped out from under her and she fell head over heels for Alexander Harper. Womanizer. Millionaire. Heartbreaker.

He kissed her, briefly but firmly right on the mouth for anyone at the stuffy gathering to see, and for once she didn't care how her parents would interpret the gesture.

"Let's get out of here." His low-pitched voice rumbled over her exposed nerve endings.

"What about working the crowd? I haven't introduced you to the mayor yet."

"Invite him to my party. I'll meet him then."

Her heart took a swan dive and landed right in a hot spring of desire. This crash was going to hurt. But she would survive it, just as she'd survived every other one.

"Lead the way."

* * *

He had to be out of his mind to leave the gala before he'd maximized the connections he'd paid good money to make.

But Alex lost enthusiasm for networking when the excitement in Amanda's eyes turned to anxiety. Sure, she had sucked it up and pasted on a smile, but the overwhelming urge to convert her smile back into a genuine one was as unexpected as it was unwanted.

He didn't need any more drama in his life. He had enough with the threat to expose Zack's paternity. Amanda's mother was a first-class drama queen. A real bitch. He'd recognized her type instantly from his frequent exposure through work. Money battles brought out the worst in most people.

If her parents were that critical it was no wonder Amanda didn't want them to know about her financial problems. Compared to his parents, who'd always put their children first and often at great personal sacrifice, Dominique Crawford's open disrespect and criticism had been hard to swallow. Alex relaxed his tensed muscles. He'd been angry on Amanda's behalf.

"I've missed holding you, Amanda." He dragged a fingernail down the tense line of her spine and relished the hitch of her breath, her shiver and the flush returning to her pale cheeks.

"You're sure you don't mind leaving early?"

The hunger he found in her gaze as she looked up at him made him suck a sharp breath. "I'm sure I'd rather be in your bed tasting you than here drinking inferior champagne."

Her lips parted, and her pink tongue appeared briefly to dampen them. The need to taste her hit him hard. But public displays of affection were not appropriate here and he'd already slipped up once. Amanda had a bad habit of edging past the steel barriers he locked around his emotions. A wise man would cut her loose and move on. But the rewards of having her by his side outweighed the risk of slipping again. She'd made a couple of introductions for him tonight that could prove lucrative if he followed up on them. And of course he would. Business always came first.

Lacing his fingers through hers, he led her toward the entrance. The time it took to retrieve their coats dragged, making him impatient to hold her. He finally got her outside in the blustery cold air, inside the wrought-iron colonnade tucked out of sight of paparazzi and gala guests. He yanked her close and covered her lips, catching her frosty breath in his mouth. Amanda opened to him instantly and kissed him back, not trying to hide her desire or temper her hunger. She tasted of champagne and her own addictive flavor.

Her fingers clutched his coat at his waist, pulling him closer. He liked that Amanda didn't play games. What she wanted, she took without apology but also without the greediness of other women he'd known, because she returned the pleasure she received tenfold. And it made him so hot he needed to shed his overcoat and grind her against the cold wall before he spontaneously incinerated. He considered dragging her the ten blocks to her apartment at a run.

Instead, he eased back and pulled in enough air to clear his head. "Your place. Now."

Her shiver shook him to the core. She spun away from him and stalked through the gates to the street.

What the— Had he offended her?

"Taxi!" she called out and he grinned. Amanda definitely didn't play games. She was bold and blunt, sometimes too blunt, like the times she'd told him to go bother someone else. But her resistance had only increased his determination to have her. She'd been well worth the battle.

A taxi cruised to a stop in front of them. Alex opened the door and followed her in, giving the cabbie her address. And then, because he couldn't resist in the privacy of the car, he pulled her into his lap. The layers of their coats and clothing did nothing to block the arousing pressure of her butt against his growing arousal—especially when she met his gaze and shifted, slowly, deliberately, to settle herself more comfortably in his lap. Desire burned through him.

She unbuttoned her coat in the hot, stuffy cab and the simple seductive releasing of the five buttons from collar to hip seemed as erotic as hell. The fabric parted, revealing the thigh-high slit in her gown and intensifying the heat in his groin.

That slit in her dress had driven him wild all evening. With each step she'd taken she'd flashed him with her mile-long legs and stiletto heels. He'd become distracted more than once with the mental image of her wearing nothing but those shoes.

Keeping his eyes on the rearview mirror to make sure the taxi driver wasn't watching, he spread his palm over her knee. Amanda's breath hitched audibly. He inched his way up her thigh, caressing her smooth, warm skin and he wondered how far he'd go. How far she'd *let* him go.

The fact that they were not alone added to the risk of discovery and heightened his excitement—not something he'd experienced before. He wasn't a PDA kind of guy. But Amanda, the craving for her mouth and the feel of her skin, was corrupting him. Waiting another five minutes to have her seemed impossible.

As his hand inched higher her breaths quickened, as did his, until he was only inches from her panties, from her appletini tattoo. He bent his head, burying his mouth and nose in her neck. He inhaled her fragrance. Not cologne. Pure Amanda. He sipped from her soft skin, swirled his tongue over the pulse pounding beneath her jaw. Her short nails dug into his thigh and her breath hissed.

His thumb eased under her silk dress, reached the crease where the elastic leg of her panties should have been and encountered…only skin and curls. Hunger for her exploded in his gut, in his groin and pulsed heavily through his veins.

Amanda's passion-filled eyes telegraphed her need in the darkened cab. Then the cab swerved, jarring him, forcing his thumb into her damp folds. His control jumped the tracks like a derailed train. He sank deeper into her slickness.

"Ten fifty," the cabbie said from the front, jarring Alex from fantasy to reality.

He reluctantly removed his hand and allowed Amanda to slide from his lap, which she did with excruciating slowness. He dug for his wallet, handed the driver a twenty and followed Amanda from the car without waiting for change. She hugged her coat around her and hustled for the glass-and-mahogany doors of 721. He followed more slowly, trying to recover his control and staggered by how close he'd come to losing it. In a cab.

This affair would have to end before he made a fool of himself. But it wasn't going to end tonight.

The doorman greeted them. But Alex didn't want to waste time in the lobby. He nodded at the man, hooked his arm around Amanda's back and hurried her toward the elevator.

Inside the car he backed her up against the wall, tucked his knee between hers and pinned her with his chest. Conscious of the security cameras and the guy watching downstairs, he reined himself in.

"You're not wearing panties," he whispered.

She smiled. Wickedly. Seductively. "No, I'm not."

He eased his hands inside her coat and around her waist and then down over her bottom, pulling her hips to his to let her feel how she affected him. The fall of her coat would conceal his actions. "If I'd known that at the gala I wouldn't have lasted five minutes."

She rolled her eyes. "Oh, please. You wouldn't have left without meeting the top ten on your list."

The accuracy of her remark surprised him. "Why would you say that?"

"Because I've watched you at every party we've attended since we met. You always have an agenda. I can almost see you ticking off your mental list. And then when you've finished it, you always come after me. The only reason you were willing to leave tonight was because you'd checked off your must-meet people before my parents arrived."

The woman was dead on target. She read him too well. "You've been watching me?"

Her gaze remained locked on his, but her cheeks pinked and her lashes fluttered over her grey eyes. "You know I have. And just so you know, my pantiless state has nothing to do with you and everything to do with the lines of the dress."

"I don't believe you."

The elevator doors opened behind him. He straightened and released her, allowing her to precede him to her door. She glanced at him over her shoulder as she pushed her key into the lock. "Believe what you want. I know the truth."

"The truth is that you want me as much as I want you."

Her sassy smile faded. "Yes, I do."

She turned away to open the door and then stepped inside. When her gaze met his again, the worry had left her eyes and the teasing tilt of her lips had returned. "The question is, what are you going to do about it, Alex?"

"This." He swept her into his arms, kicked her door closed and carried her straight through to her bedroom. Once he reached the side of her bed he shoved off her coat. The garment and her evening purse hit the floor. He wanted her naked. Now. And he wanted inside her. He dropped his own overcoat and tux jacket and reached for his tie. The fabric snagged and refused to loosen.

She batted his hands away, untying the knotted snarl he'd made of the black bow tie. Next she started on his shirt, releasing one button at a time and then yanking it from his pants and shoving it from his shoulders. Her short nails scraped down his chest, dredging up a firestorm of need and making his muscles jump.

When her fingers hooked behind his waistband, he sucked a lungful of air, caught her hands and put them by her side. Too much. Too soon. He studied her dress, found the zipper down the side of the curve-hugging, strapless red gown and eased it south. Her clothing fell to the floor, leaving her bare except for her heels.

He clamped his teeth on a groan. Seeing her naked

never failed to deflate his lungs. He fought for breath, for control, for reason. Amanda made him lose his head.

She smiled, scooped up her garments and strolled across her room to drape coat and dress over a chair. She was teasing, stalling, but he savored every wiggle of her hips, and he'd bet she had added that extra sway to her gait because she knew his gaze was glued to her incredible rear view. Amanda was long and lean, but curved where it counted. The woman had the kind of butt made to wear a thong…or nothing at all.

And then she pivoted, slowly, like a runway model. He drank in her breasts, their nipples tight and waiting for his hands, for his mouth. His gaze rolled over her narrow waist, the tattoo on her hip near the pale blond triangle of curls and down those mind-wrecking legs. His hands fisted against the need to grab her and toss her on the mattress.

Looking at her creamy skin from a distance wasn't enough. He kicked off his shoes and shed his attire with record-breaking haste. When he was bare she strolled back toward him with a hips-rolling, make-his-tongue-hang-out stride. Her eyes telegraphed her desire, exponentially increasing his own.

How did she reduce him to testosterone insanity so easily? But she'd had that effect on him from the first day they'd met. Even after she'd told him to get lost. *Especially* after she'd told him to get lost. Women who knew his income bracket and background didn't push him away. But wanting Amanda was more than just the need to acquire what he'd been denied.

She lifted a hand toward his face. He captured it and carried her wrist to his lips. Stringing a trail of kisses up her pale inner arm, past her elbow, to the tender skin of her bicep, he relished each gasp and each shudder he wrenched from her. He enjoyed the heavy fall of her lashes drifting across her cheeks and the warmth of her skin against his lips. He savored her taste on his tongue.

Amanda draped her arm around his neck and stepped into his embrace, the way she'd done on the dance floor tonight, only now his tux and her dress weren't between them.

Her flesh curved into his, searing him. Her flat belly brushed his erection, sending a megawatt of electricity charging through his system. She swayed against him, as if dancing to a tune playing in her head, and he could barely breathe, barely think, barely stand.

When she lifted her lips, he didn't refuse the invitation. Her mouth was soft, her tongue wild. The ravenous kiss consumed what was left of his control. He swept her into his arms and eased her onto the bed, following her down and blanketing her with his body. The funky, fuzzy fabric of her comforter tickled his knees and shins and forearms. But it was the slick welcome of her body that blew all but one of his fuses.

Damn. Damn. Damn. How did she make him forget the most basic rules? He withdrew. "Condom."

Amanda twisted beneath him, opened the small carved jewelry box on her nightstand and withdrew a condom packet. She'd been keeping them there since he'd started sleeping over.

Palming his chest, she shoved him back until he knelt between her knees and then she planted kisses along his hipbone while applying the protection. Her tongue licked a path of fire along his flesh, making his stomach muscles quiver while her hand stroked latex down his rigid shaft.

He gritted his teeth against the jolt of pleasure but a groan seeped through.

Reclining again, she opened her arms and smiled that smile at him—the one that made steam rise from his pores. He loved that she'd turned a stupid mistake into sexy foreplay. But that was Amanda. She had a way of pulling something unexpected to keep him on his toes. A guy could get used to that. If he'd let himself.

But he wouldn't. He couldn't.

He bent and kissed her hard and fast on the mouth, but then slowed his pace as he strung nips and kisses down her neck, over her collarbone, from one nipple to the other. She writhed beneath him as he made his way down the center of her abdomen, past her navel, to the swollen flesh buried in her curls. He sucked her bud into his mouth and flicked it with his tongue. Her flavor registered simultaneously with her moan.

He alternated laving her, sucking her and gently nibbling until her knees bent and her back bowed—the sign he'd been waiting for that told him she was clinging to the edge. He freed her to rise up so he could sink deep inside her. Slick and hot and wet, she surrounded him. He withdrew, returned, withdrew again and then he reached between them and stroked her.

Release crashed over her, contracting her internal muscles around him and filling his ears with her cries of pleasure. He struggled to make it last. Sweat broke out on his skin as he brought her to orgasm a second and third time. He started to shake with the effort of holding back, and then her lids lifted. Smoky grey eyes caught and held his as she reached out and hooked his nape with her hand. She dragged his mouth to hers and bit his bottom lip then sucked it into her mouth. And blew his restraint straight to hell. He couldn't pull back. Couldn't dam the flood of pleasure.

Orgasm pounded through him, slamming him with wave after blinding wave of sensation. When it finally ended, he collapsed to his elbows over her. Winded. Drained. Sated.

Her lips curved into a satisfied smile and something wrenched in his chest. That's when it hit him.

It was going to be hard to let Amanda Crawford go.

Eight

Heart pounding, Amanda dropped her PDA back into her briefcase Monday morning, reached for her desk calendar and counted back again. But modern technology hadn't failed. The numbers didn't change on paper.

Her period was late.

Not late enough to panic. Yet. She'd give it another day or two. And then she'd panic. If she had to.

Which she wouldn't.

But you're never late.

She took several calming breaths and reminded herself there was a first time for everything. And being late didn't have to mean anything. She'd been under a lot of stress lately. And stress messed up body clocks, didn't it?

But what if it wasn't stress, the nagging voice in her head insisted. How could a slip like this have happened? When had she and Alex ever not used protection? She searched her memories of the hot, steamy, slow and fast encounters and—

The first time. That first time in her bedroom they hadn't used a condom.

Her stomach sank at the memory. She braced herself against the kitchen counter. How could they have been so stupid? And how could she not have thought about it even once since that day two weeks ago? She was never careless about birth control or safe sex. Never.

She pressed her hands to her belly and gulped for air.

She couldn't afford a baby. She could barely support herself, and until she had her financial mess unraveled—

The bathroom door opened, severing her thoughts. She lowered her hands. Steam billowed out, followed by Alex wearing only a lavender towel low around his hips. The feminine color did nothing to lessen the masculine impact of his broad shoulders, ripped abs and long, muscular legs. Her pulse kicked erratically in appreciation.

No matter how strong her reservations, after Friday night at her place they'd spent the entire weekend together in Greenwich. When they'd managed to climb out of bed, he'd taken her to Round Hill, an old Continental Army lookout point with a great view of the Manhattan skyline. They'd strolled hand in hand past the exclusive boutiques and restaurants of Greenwich Avenue, people watching, window-shopping and discussing alternative venues for Zack's party. The Harpers' home was still an option, but Amanda had wanted to come up with something more special for Zack's big day.

Alex hadn't left after returning Amanda to her apartment last night. She hadn't been able to get enough of his company. She might as well admit it. She was putty in his hands. What Alex wanted, Alex got. Eventually. From her, anyway. How she'd held out as long as she had was a miracle.

But this...

She opened her mouth to spill the bad news, and then closed it again. Why ruin his day on a maybe? She'd worry enough for both of them. She'd take a pregnancy test first. And then she'd tell him *if* there was anything to tell.

There wouldn't be.

He walked toward her, stopping a foot away. "I'll be tied up in court all day and I have a client dinner tonight."

"That's okay. I have several appointments today and I'll be very late getting home." Her level tone pleased her. No trace of panic tinged her words. She hoped her expression didn't give away her tormented concerns.

He finger-combed his damp hair. His biceps and pectoral muscles flexed, and his towel slipped down, revealing an inch of the thick dark hair in his groin. He looked so sexy her mouth watered and her internal muscles clenched. She struggled with the urge to stroke her fingertips down his still damp chest.

"Then I'll head for Greenwich tonight." He stroked her jaw line. "Unless you want to give me a key."

Shock knocked her back a step. "No."

That hadn't sounded good. She'd practically shouted at him, and from the tightening of his lips, he wasn't crazy about her reaction. But she couldn't repeat the mistake she'd made with Curtis and Douglas of trusting too much. Both men had cost her self-respect and cash. She didn't think she'd ever trust a man enough to give him access to her home or her heart again.

"I'm sorry, Alex. I don't want to go there. We're temporary. Remember?"

He didn't correct her.

Did you want him to?

No.

Maybe.

After a tense silence he nodded. Even though he hadn't moved, he'd withdrawn so far he might as well be standing on the opposite side of the room. "I'll call you in the morning."

"The masks I ordered are due to arrive tomorrow. I'll stop by to get your approval. I'll check with Moira for a good time first."

"That will work." His dark gaze ran over her lime tunic sweater and black miniskirt, tights and boots. And with just that slow look he quickened her pulse and her respiratory rate and turned her insides into a jumble. "You seem in a hurry to get out the door. I'll lock up if you're gone when I get through dressing."

Avoiding an awkward good-bye appealed on so many levels.

"Thank you." So formal. They spoke like acquaintances rather than a couple who'd been entwined like mating snakes less than an hour ago.

But then Alex had withdrawn immediately after making love to her last night. She'd fully expected him to make an excuse and leave. But he hadn't. And this morning he'd reached for her again, but put that same distance between them after satisfying her so many times could barely walk on her wobbly legs. He hadn't joined her in the shower—a first since he'd started staying over.

What did that mean?

He probably had his mind on work. He'd mentioned a complicated case going to trial this week. Or with his party only five days away, maybe he was prioritizing that who-he-must-connect-with list. Because even though this was a company party, he'd invited quite a few influential outsiders.

Whatever the cause of his tension, she wasn't going to increase it by blurting out her fears. She'd stop by the pharmacy and pick up a pregnancy test on the way back from her morning appointment. She could take the test tonight…or tomorrow…or maybe she'd just wait a few more days to make the purchase. She was probably jumping the gun anyway. Why even waste money on the test?

Coward.

He took a step toward her. She planted a palm on his chest and his heat seeped up her arm and into her core. She was too rattled to handle another one of his meltdown kisses at the moment.

"We'd both better get going if we don't want to be late."

She had absolutely no idea how Alex would react to the situation. If there was a situation. Would he want a child? Would he pressure her into having it if she didn't want to? Did she want to have a baby even though it would totally mess up her life at the moment?

Boy, wouldn't your parents love an illegitimate grandchild?

Not.

So not only did she have to find out if she was pregnant, she had to decide whether or not to share the test results with Alex. Not doing so seemed devious and underhanded. But telling him and knowing his ability to talk her into almost anything…

His hand covered hers, his fingers laced through hers and then he lifted their linked hands to his mouth. He nibbled on the fleshy pad at the base of her thumb and her hormones went haywire. Darn him, he knew that made her knees week.

Her heart raced. She snatched her hand away and cleared her throat. "Well, then, have a great day. I'll see you tomorrow."

She scooped up her coat and briefcase and bolted. There were decisions she just couldn't handle at the moment. Later, when she was dealing with facts instead of just terrifying, life-altering possibilities, she'd be more mature. But at the moment she felt more like a hysterical eighteen-year-old than a mature woman of twenty-eight.

"Moira had to step out for a moment," the Harper & Associates receptionist told Amanda on Tuesday afternoon. "You're welcome to go back to Mr. Harper's private waiting room if you'd like."

Becoming a frequent visitor to Harper & Associates evidently carried some perks. She was now trusted to go places without an escort.

"Thank you. I will." Amanda wheeled the rolling attaché down the hall and into the now-familiar room. She shed her coat, hung it in Moira's closet and crossed to her favorite chair tucked out of the way in the corner. But she was too agitated to sit.

Instead, she walked to the window. Worry churned in her stomach as it had been doing since her discovery yesterday morning. She'd found the courage to buy the pregnancy test kit, but chickened out before using it and hid it beneath her bathroom cabinet where she wouldn't have to look at it until she was ready to take the plunge. She hated her cowardice, but reminded herself a day or two's delay wouldn't change the outcome.

Focusing on a tourist helicopter in the distance, she tried to block out her personal mental clutter and concentrate on business—the one area of her life that was mostly under control thanks to Alex's loan. She'd brought an assortment of the Mardi Gras party favors for Alex's approval. It was merely a formality. She didn't expect him to object to any of the materials. Her favorite supplier had done its usual top-notch job.

Alex's office door opened, and the anticipation of seeing him raced through her like a lit fuse. She really needed to work on putting some emotional distance between them, but her heart wasn't receiving the message.

A svelte, expensively dressed and glammed-up redhead strode into the opening, stopped and turned back to the room she'd vacated. "I'm glad you called, Alex. It's good to see you again. I've missed you."

She had a smoky, sultry voice and her tone was far too intimate for a client/lawyer conversation.

Prickles of unease tickled Amanda's nape like a spiderweb.

"Keep this between us," Alex's deep baritone said, as he stepped into view. He didn't look Amanda's way.

"You know I'll do that. For you, I'd do *any*thing."

Amanda's spine snapped straighter at the emphasis on *any*. The woman's body language said she wasn't talking about bringing him chicken soup when he had a cold. Her pale fingers with red-tipped nails caressed his black lapel and then adjusted his ruby tie. And he let her. This man who didn't like PDAs let the woman mess with him. Never mind it was his private office.

"I don't want this to get out," he added.

"Neither do I."

Alex's visitor rose on tiptoe, cupped his cheek and then kissed the corner of his mouth. She lingered far too long for Amanda's peace of mind, and then Amanda's worry turned into something ugly and uncomfortable and shocking. Something that made her need a stiff drink or three.

Jealousy? Was she *jealous* of Alex and this woman? She couldn't be. That emotion implied deeper feelings— the kind of feelings that led to wanting something…permanent. And painful.

She wasn't ready for that and probably never would be.

She studied Alex and the woman. Their familiarity implied there was definitely something between them. But what? A current relationship? History? Whatever their connection, the woman wanted more of it. She wanted Alex. That desire was evident in every line of her seductively garbed body.

Had Alex decided to move on when Amanda refused to give him a key yesterday? For all she knew he might have an entire ring of women's keys. He'd certainly asked for hers easily enough. And hadn't Julia warned her repeatedly of his reputation as a player? That was one of the main reasons Amanda had avoided him so long.

"So about tonight…" the redhead purred, looking up at him through her lashes.

Pain stabbed Amanda in her chest. She gasped. Alex had claimed he had another business dinner tonight. Had he lied?

He turned and spotted her. A trace of red lipstick lingered on his skin. "Amanda."

She felt used, discarded, hurt. Betrayed. He had a date tonight and he'd lied to her. Struggling for composure and clinging desperately to her pride, she squared her shoulders. "I'm here for our appointment."

"Chelsea, you know the way out." His dark gaze never left Amanda's. Amanda made a painful note of the lack of introduction. Who was this woman Alex didn't want her to meet?

"Of course I do, since I come here so often." The coquettish tone returned.

The witch's barb hit the target again. Amanda fought to conceal the hurt. But she couldn't help wondering if she'd gotten herself possibly pregnant by a two-timing, womanizing jerk. And if she had, then what?

The woman left, but the ache in Amanda's heart didn't lessen and the knot in her stomach intensified with each passing second.

There was only one possible cause for her current misery. She'd fallen for Alex Harper, womanizer extraordinaire. To make matters worse, she might be carrying his baby.

Her parents were going to love this.

"I'm glad you're here, Amanda. Come in."

Alex's words made her jump. How could she tell him about her pregnancy concerns now? She couldn't. Not today. Maybe never. Was there even anything to tell? She prayed there wasn't. Her child—if there was one— deserved better than a guy who juggled women like a day trader does stocks and bonds.

Concentrate on the job, Amanda.

She forced her limbs into motion, snatched the handle

of the rolling attaché in a knuckle-numbing grip and dragged the case into his inner sanctum. The room smelled like him and *her*. A trace of the woman's heavy cologne lingered. The corner of his desk where Amanda and Alex had almost made love—*had sex*—pulled her gaze like a magnet. Had Alex and the redhead—

Never ask a question to which you don't want to know the answer.

Redirecting her attention to the task at hand, she flipped open the latches of the case and very carefully laid a representative assortment of masks and beads across his desk. She couldn't think of a word to say. She dredged her brain for the reason for her visit and finally pulled a few thoughts together.

"Take a look at these samples. If they're not right I can reorder by five this evening to get replacements in time for Saturday's event."

"Amanda." He cupped her shoulder. She jumped out of reach.

"Don't."

His eyebrows lowered. "What's wrong?"

"When I'm in an intimate relationship I am exclusive. For health reasons I refuse to share."

His eyes narrowed. "What are you implying?"

The red smear drew her gaze like a light does moths. "You're wearing her lipstick."

He removed a handkerchief from his inner pocket, wiped the telltale spot, then looked at the stained cloth. "Chelsea and I are not together."

"I don't believe you."

His shoulders snapped back. "I won't waste my time trying to convince you."

"Who is she?"

He seemed to weigh his response carefully. "Someone I knew years ago. We were involved, but we aren't any longer."

That qualified as an evasive answer. "Not by her choice."

"Chelsea has always wanted what she couldn't have."

And Chelsea wanted Alex. Her make-him-notice clothing and do-me-now heels made her intentions to entice him abundantly clear. Had Alex been tempted? While he hadn't kissed the witch back, he hadn't moved away, either.

Amanda rolled a shoulder, feigning disinterest. "Whatever. But from now on you and I are business only. I won't sleep with you anymore."

Because she couldn't share a man she'd fallen in love with. *Love.* The admission sent another round of aftershocks through her. How had this happened? She didn't want to fall in love. She sucked at it. Her three previous relationships were proof of that.

She turned away quickly and straightened the rows of party junk on his desk. Her hands were far from steady and no matter how hard she tried she couldn't stop the tremor. She hoped Alex didn't notice.

He moved into her peripheral vision. "What about our agreement?"

Dread curdled in her stomach. She stilled her frantic rearranging and risked looking at him. "Which agreement? The loan? You told me there were no strings attached."

"I'm talking about our mutually beneficial introductions and you hosting my parties."

Her heart was ripping in two and all he cared about were his stupid parties? Her throat burned and nausea decided to make an unwelcome cameo appearance. She was so tired of being used by the ill-chosen men in her life. And so sick of choosing unwisely. She had to work on that.

Forget it. Go back to the no-men rule for a decade or two.

"I'll do what you paid me to do. But no more."

He lifted a hand and stroked her cheek before she could jerk out of reach. The brief contact hit her like a Taser, locking her muscles and jamming her thoughts so she couldn't escape.

"We're good together, Amanda."

She had to get out of here before she lost it. "And we still will be. On a professional level."

Unwilling to take the time to wait for him to examine the samples or to repack her attaché case, she backed toward the door. She wouldn't need that case again before Saturday anyway. She only used it when she had heavy stuff to lug around.

"Have a look at the masks, beads and other party favors. If you want any changes then have Moira call me by four-thirty this afternoon. I'll fax any other pertinent information to you between now and Saturday. I have another appointment." *Liar.* "I have to go."

The pain on Amanda's face ripped Alex apart. He didn't want her to leave. Not yet. Not like this. He wanted to tell her the truth. All of it. The realization made him uneasy. He'd never wanted to share Zack's parentage with anyone except Zack. The risk for his son to get hurt was too high. But with the threat of blowing the Harper family's privacy to hell hanging over his head, he wanted Amanda to hear it from him first.

The urge to share didn't mean he was falling for her. He only needed Amanda's opinion on how to handle the situation. The police and his parents were giving him no help. And he wanted Amanda to stay and wash away the stench of Chelsea's self-absorbed personality.

Amanda was as open and honest as Chelsea was devious and conniving. Amanda would never lie to him or keep something from him the way Chelsea had eighteen years ago when her actions had robbed him of the power to make a decision that had affected the rest of his life, the rest of Zack's life. He would never ever let a woman do that to him again.

"Stay." Besides the off-the-Richter-Scale sex, he enjoyed Amanda's company. Too much? Probably. But he had to love—*like,* he amended—a woman who not only understood the intricacies of football but could also throw on a designer gown and network like a pro before stripping down to skin and driving him out of his mind.

The novelty of their attraction would eventually burn out, but he'd had three calls already as a result of Amanda's introductions Friday night. He didn't intend to let her go this soon.

Shaking her head, she backed toward the door. "I can't."

"You asked Moira to block off thirty minutes."

"Something came up." There was an unfamiliar quiver in her voice and she wouldn't meet his gaze. A strange idea implanted itself in his head and wouldn't let go.

"Are you jealous of Chelsea?"

She jerked and stared at him as if he'd said something insane. "Jealous? Why would I be jealous? We're temporary, remember? I told you at the beginning that I didn't want anything more from you."

The statement should have filled him with relief. Temporary was his MO. Instead, her words left him feeling…off balance. He searched for a firmer footing, lifted a hand and traced her jawline with his fingertip. The hitch of her breath rewarded his efforts. He loved touching her soft, smooth, satiny skin.

"We are a potent and effective combination."

She stepped out of reach. "You're a client. I should never have let this become personal. From here on out we'll focus on our professional relationship and you can go back to your Chelseas. It was only a matter of time before you did anyway, Alex."

She yanked open his door and stormed out. He wasn't ready to let her go. He strode after her.

"Alex," Moira called out. "Bill Hines is on line one."

Hines would be Harper & Associates' largest corporate account—if Alex could land him. Torn between work and following Amanda, Alex stopped in his waiting area. His gaze followed Amanda down the hall, but duty turned his feet away from the door.

Business always came first. Success meant power. And he could never get enough of that.

But for the first time he wanted to say to hell with the climb to the top.

Nine

Amanda focused on Julia's rounded belly and sent up a silent prayer that she wouldn't be in the same situation in a few months.

Not that she had anything against children. She'd never really thought much about having them. The idea of getting married and having a family had always been a hazy, distant "someday" possibility. But the present timing couldn't have been worse. She prayed this was a false alarm. But deep in her heart she suspected it wasn't.

She fluffed her hair and shifted her gaze from Julia's stomach to her so-radiant-it-hurt-to-look-at face and then back to her plate. The two of them had elected to sit on the floor and eat at the coffee table, but Amanda's favorite food just wasn't ringing her chimes tonight.

How could two intelligent college graduates both end

up accidentally pregnant? That just didn't happen in the real world.

Okay, it did. But not to her.

Please don't let it be happening to me.

She needed someone to talk to. Her whole sordid story hovered on the tip of her tongue, but she just couldn't find the courage to confess her worries to Julia. Not yet.

"Are you okay?" Julia asked.

Amanda blinked—innocently, she hoped—at her friend. "Why wouldn't I be?"

"You're very quiet. That's not like you."

"I'm a little distracted by Alex's party." And the late period. And Alex. And the fact that she really missed having him in her bed…and her body.

She couldn't remember ever having something she couldn't share with her friend, and when she'd come over to Max and Julia's penthouse loft for a girls' night of take-out Chinese, she'd been determined to discuss the situation and her options.

She knew Julia wouldn't judge or condemn her because her former roommate had been caught in exactly the same position. Julia's pregnancy hadn't been planned, either. It had been the result of a passionate one-night stand with Max seven months ago. Julia had already had to swim through those murky "what if/what'll I do" waters. She'd since married the father of her baby and couldn't possibly be happier, if her glowing face was an indicator.

But marrying Alex wasn't an option for Amanda. She sucked at relationships, had lousy judgment in the male selection department and was a rotten example of not-so-happily-ever-after to her parents. Not to mention, Alex wasn't interested in marriage. And then there were her money issues, her determination to avoid workaholics like her father and—

Don't dwell on shortcomings.

Hard not to when the list is so long.

Even though she knew Julia would offer her unbiased guidance, Amanda wasn't ready to share her secret. For pity's sake, she couldn't even bring herself to use the test kit until she knew where she stood with Alex.

Was she on her own in this decision? Or not?

Was the redhead a factor…or wasn't she?

Julia rubbed her tummy. "Is Alex staying out of your hair and out of your bed?"

Amanda jerked in surprise. Her kung pao chicken fell from her chopsticks and landed with a splat in her lap. Oops. Life had been so hectic she hadn't filled Julia in on the status change over the past two weeks.

"Um. Alex is Alex. He's never going to change," she hedged, and snatched up a paper napkin to blot at the mess clinging to her sweater—more to avoid Julia's perceptive blue eyes than to clean what was probably going to be a permanent stain.

"Well, yes, but his interest in you has outlived any of his other relationships that I've heard about."

"Probably because I didn't fall all over him." In the beginning. She searched for a safer topic. "The RSVPs are rolling in, but I'm surprised some of our neighbors haven't responded. I haven't heard from Carrie and Trent or Sebastian and Tessa."

"That's because they're all out of the country. Carrie and Trent are on a prewedding honeymoon in Caspia. They won't be back in time to attend."

Disappointed, Amanda frowned. How could she

have missed that her second-floor neighbors weren't even in the building? Had the affair with Alex filled her head with smog?

"A *pre*wedding honeymoon? Isn't that a little backward? Honeymoons come *after* the wedding for most people." Although she had no room to object if her neighbors did things a little out of proper order. She could be the poster child for bending rules. Besides, thinking outside the box was a requirement for a good party planner.

"Prince Sebastian and his fiancée Tessa gave Carrie and Trent the trip as a wedding gift, and Sebastian and Tessa are over there with them, showing them around the country. We have very generous neighbors." The wistful tone of the last phrase caught Amanda by surprise.

"Do you miss living at 721?"

"Yes and no. I miss you and our friends, but not the intrigue. And I have Max. His place isn't too shabby," she added, with a twinkle in her eyes.

"No. Not shabby at all." Amanda's gaze swept the large room with its wide-planked oak floors, a fireplace flanked by loaded bookcases and the oversize furniture. Julia's new digs couldn't be more comfy and inviting. "And soon you'll have your baby."

"Not soon enough."

A buzz from the intercom interrupted them. Julia lumbered to her feet, crossed the room and pushed the button. "Yes?"

"Julia, buzz me in." Alex's deep voice filled the room. Amanda's stomach plunged.

"I need to see Amanda," he continued.

Wide-eyed and near panic, Amanda shook her head vigorously. She wasn't ready to see him today. This afternoon's introduction to jealousy had rattled her cage. She'd never been jealous before. Ever. And she didn't like it. Not at all.

Why not? Julia mouthed silently.

Too much to explain. Again, Amanda shook her head and held up her hands in the universal stop sign.

Julia sighed and turned back to the intercom. "What makes you think she's here?"

"Max told me."

Amanda winced. Max had been nice enough to clear out and let them have a girls' night, but this killed any gratitude she might have felt toward him.

"You can come up." Julia pushed the door release button. She turned to Amanda. "I'm not going to lie to him. He's Max's best friend. Do you want to tell me why you're avoiding Alex? Or should I ask him?"

Amanda debated for thirty seconds before admitting defeat. Julia would never let her out of the loft without a total confession. "We were sleeping together. Now we're not. I'm late. And I think he's two-timing me with a gorgeous redhead."

Julia's mouth dropped open at the rushed summation. She sagged against the wall beside the door. "Couldn't you have mentioned this earlier instead of chitchatting about nursery colors?"

Amanda grimaced. "I should have, but I—I didn't know where to start. And now I don't know what to do." A knock halted her words. Alex was here. The urge to run sent a boost of adrenaline through her muscles. But Julia wasn't giving her the option of avoiding him.

Julia reached for the doorknob but paused and pointed an imperious finger. "You're not leaving tonight until I get every detail. And I mean *every* one. You've been holding out on me."

Resignation settled over Amanda. There were some things you just had to endure, like trips to the dentist, visits with the parents and getting grilled by best friends. Thoroughly unpleasant, but survivable.

She rose from her seat on the floor and wiped her hands down her thighs. Inhaling deeply, Amanda braced herself. "Okay."

Julia nodded and opened the door.

There was no way for Amanda to prepare for the impact of Alex's dark gaze slamming into hers. For several hammering heartbeats, he stared and she couldn't breathe or move her locked muscles, and then he glanced away briefly to greet Julia before turning back to Amanda. "We need to talk."

She wet her lips and swallowed in a futile attempt to ease her dry mouth. "I think we've said all there is to say."

"Now, Amanda." His firm, inflexible voice made her wonder if he had a bit of a stubborn streak. But then what male didn't? And he had been as persistent as a pigeon in Central Park in chasing her. So yes, he definitely had a stubborn streak.

But she wasn't going have this conversation in front of Julia. Amanda reluctantly walked toward him. "Not here. Outside."

"Wait," Julia called out. "You are not leaving. I'll give you some privacy."

As much as Amanda appreciated the support, she wanted to handle this situation her way, and that meant not telling Alex about her late period yet. Maybe she'd tell him after his party. If it was still necessary. But Julia had no way of knowing that and she might unintentionally blurt out something.

Amanda shook her head. "We're just going to step out for a moment. I'll be back to finish our dinner. I promise."

Not that she expected to be able to put another bite in her churning stomach. But she'd promised to give Julia details and she would keep her promise.

Alex held the door for her and then followed her out into the hall. For several seconds his dark eyes pinned her in place, probing, seeking, wanting. Oh, yes, the want was there plain to see and it kindled a reciprocal need in Amanda.

Tension stretched between them. Tension and awareness. A trace of his cologne underlain by his own scent teased her senses, and her clothing suddenly weighed heavily on her overly sensitized skin. Every breath dragged the fabric over her like a caress.

How could she still desire him if he'd two-timed her? Had she no brains whatsoever? No self-preservation instinct? No pride? Sure, he'd claimed there was nothing between him and the redhead, but she'd seen the connection.

She refused to squirm or look away from him. Instead, she folded her arms and leaned back against the wall, feigning calm she wasn't even close to experiencing. If she managed to bluff her way through this confrontation she wouldn't have to see him again except at his party and his brother's. The rest of the details could be phoned in.

Her heart would have time to heal. And she'd have time to make decisions.

"Alex, what could possibly be so important that you had to tell me in person rather than call or send me an e-mail?"

Moving as fast as a striking snake, he planted a hand on the wall on either side of her head and then his mouth covered hers. Shock held her immobile for a few heart-beats while his lips plied hers with a skill she'd come to appreciate and crave, and then her brain kicked in.

How dare he! She shoved against his chest, but instead of moving away he slowly bent his elbows, closing the gap between them. The weight and heat of his body ironed her flat against the wall, trapping her hands between them. His heart beat rock-steady, if somewhat rapidly, against her palms. His hips and thighs nudged hers.

Hunger rumbled to life inside her and she couldn't kill it any more than she could slow her quickening pulse or keep her lips sealed when he stroked them apart. His tongue twined with hers, slick and seductive, familiar and arousing. He coaxed a response from her that she was shockingly willing to give. Her heart raced and heat flooded her.

How could she give this up? She'd never been so physically in tune with a man before. Her hands slid to his shoulders and then his nape. Supple skin and soft hair teased her fingertips. She stroked his jaw, savoring his evening beard.

He lifted his head slightly. "You can't e-mail this."

Before she could gather her wits and escape, his lips returned with devastating, protest-robbing results. So much for resisting. He sucked her bottom lip between his teeth, nipping it lightly before easing back until only their foreheads and the tips of their noses touched. "We shouldn't be doing this."

"You can try to deny the chemistry between us, Amanda, but it's not going to work. We are a dynamic team. In bed and out. I'm not letting you go. Not yet."

Reason rallied slowly, kicked into gear by a weak wave of indignation. "You can't make me keep seeing you."

"Is that a challenge?"

The glint in his eyes sent a warning shiver over her. She was already on shaky ground. She didn't need to goad him. "No. It's a statement of fact. One you know as a lawyer not to cross."

He eased back a few more inches, allowing her precious breathing and thinking room. "How many calls have you had as a result of our night at the gala?"

Smart man. He hit her in the weakest spot of her dump-him-and-run argument. But then she'd never doubted Alex's intelligence. They were a good team. And it wasn't his fault her feelings had crossed the lines they'd established.

"Four," she confessed reluctantly.

His dark eyes said I told you so. He caught her chin in his fingers and forced her to meet his gaze. "Chelsea is not an issue."

The need to believe him almost overcame her good sense. "Then tell me who she is. Because it's as clear as Waterford crystal that you've slept with her."

Shadows filled his eyes. "It's not my story to tell. Others could be hurt. But we haven't been intimate in over a decade."

She searched his steady eyes, his face. Was she being stupidly gullible? Probably. Silently calling herself a fool, she conceded defeat. "I believe you."

"Then we're still a team."

A statement. Not a question.

She inhaled slowly, deeply, praying for the strength to refuse him and finding none. "We're still a team. For now."

But would her secret—her possible secret—turn him against her?

* * *

"I'll have a hard time keeping my hands off you tonight." Alex's comment from behind her in the opulent Trianon suite startled Amanda seconds before his warm, firm grip settled on her waist. He pulled her back against his muscled frame.

She tried and failed to suppress her body's spontaneous-combustion reaction to him and neutralized her expression. Using the process of turning to face him to her advantage, she stepped out of his grasp, but it was too late. The heat of his touch had branded her.

With his broad shoulders and lean build Alex looked totally edible in his black custom-tailored tux with a snowy white shirt and black tie.

She'd tried to get him to wear a colored bow tie to go with the festive Mardi Gras mood, but he wasn't the wild-colors type. And honestly, the stark black and white worked extremely well on him. It also reminded her that while she might be something of a free spirit, he was essentially conservative and traditional.

Except in bed. She quickly snuffed that thought but not soon enough to prevent a flicker of arousal from igniting at her core.

His conservative tendency was just one more reason they should not have a child together. They'd argue constantly on how to raise it. Like her parents had argued about her. In the end she hadn't fit in with either of their blueprints for her life and she'd disappointed them both. There was nothing like continuous, disappointed scowling to put a damper on life.

"Alex, the dress is beautiful. Thank you." She stroked a hand over the metallic ombré silk of the evening gown.

"You're welcome. It suits you." His appreciative gaze poured over her like heated massage oil, reinforcing his statement.

"I couldn't have chosen a more perfect dress for myself if I'd tried."

When the delivery man had handed her the box yesterday Amanda had thought her mother was up to her old tricks again, and she had come very close to refusing to accept the package. But then she'd caved and opened the lid for a quick peek, fully intending to return the garment. It had been love at first sight—even before she'd found the card from Alex tucked inside.

While her mother always sent dresses intended to showcase the Dominique apparel line's newest designs, Alex had bought a dress that made the most of Amanda's physical assets. The plunging surplice bodice enhanced her smallish bust and the empire waist and hip-molding skirt accentuated her height and slender build. A slit from the hem to her upper thigh opened when she walked and flashed her legs and silver heels.

"I adore the colors." Almost as much as she adored the man who'd chosen the dress. *Don't go there.*

To distract herself from that unwelcome thought, she glanced sideways at her reflection in the tall, arched gold-leaf mirror on the wall behind the reception table. The fabric of the bodice was a pale lavender—the exact shade of the orchid on her bedside table. The color graduated to darker shades as if the hem had wicked up a deep, luscious midnight-sky purple.

"Turn around."

Amanda hesitated at Alex's low-voiced command, but then complied when his hands cupped her shoulders and tried to turn her to face the mirror. She instinctively resisted, but reminded herself she was working for him tonight and that meant doing what he asked—within reason. She pivoted. He removed his hands, reached into his pocket and then lowered a glittering gold chain around her neck. A large briolette-cut amethyst settled between her breasts and the cool metal rested on her skin.

"A perfect match to the dress." His fingers teased her nape as he fastened the clasp sending a shiver of awareness down her spine.

She met his gaze in the mirror. "Alex, you shouldn't have."

His lips touched the side of her neck and her pulse skittered wildly. Her heart hiccuped even faster when his teeth grazed the cord of her neck. "You worked hard. You deserve it."

She'd never be able to resist him if he kept this up. She clutched the stone in her fingers and once more pulled away from the sensory overload Alex induced, and faced him. "It's my job."

Holding her gaze, he stroked her cheek with his fingertips and she all but melted at the approval in his eyes. "It's more than your job. You live for the thrill of pulling all the details together, the same way I do with a complicated court case. And you're very good at what you do, Amanda."

How could he make her stomach flip-flop with nothing more than a few kind words and a hot glance? It was disgusting how easily he aroused her.

"Thank you. For the compliments and the necklace."

Flustered and pleased, she reached across the table for the plain black half mask she'd purchased for him. "Your guests should start arriving any moment. Put this on."

His fingers brushed hers as he accepted the molded fabric and a sliver of need worked its way up her spine.

"Our guests. We're going to wow them tonight." He dragged a knuckle down her bare arm, leaving a crop of goose bumps in his wake.

She dampened her lips and reached for her white, feathered and sequined mask. She'd been hustling around all afternoon trying to put the finishing touches on the gala setup. But the hardest work was done now. Every detail had been checked and double-checked. That left her with nothing to keep her from dwelling on how much she desired the man in front of her and how complicated their lives would get if the pregnancy test delivered the wrong answer.

Don't think about that tonight.

You are the queen of denial.

She slipped on her mask and studied Alex in his. The masks immediately kicked up the naughty factor. Through the small openings Alex's brown eyes glittered with excitement, anticipation and hunger. The latter sent a ripple of awareness over her and made her wish they had a few minutes to explore whatever it was that mischievous twinkle implied. Her pulse quickened.

Approaching voices provided a grounding distraction. Alex blinked, and instantly what she'd come to recognize as his professional face replaced the passion.

Reed and Elizabeth Wellington, Amanda's neighbors who resided in one of the two penthouses at 721 Park, rounded the corner looking as wrapped up in each other as newlyweds. They didn't appear to notice Amanda or Alex until they were only a few yards away. The couple hadn't looked nearly as happy at the fifth anniversary party Amanda had organized for them last month at Cipriani

42nd Street, but tonight Elizabeth's face glowed with happiness. Being pregnant certainly agreed with Elizabeth.

"Hello, Amanda. Alex." Elizabeth kissed Amanda's cheek and gave her a quick hug, then did the same to Alex. It was almost as if Elizabeth couldn't contain her joy.

Amanda air-kissed Reed's cheek after the men shook hands. "How's Lucas?"

"He's a great kid," Reed replied. "He's ten months old now."

In addition to welcoming their own baby in seven months, the couple was in the process of adopting Elizabeth's nephew after the death of the child's parents. The process hadn't been smooth sailing, but judging by their expressions, whatever headaches they'd been through had been well worth it.

Amanda indicated the table displaying the Mardi Gras masks. "We're glad you could make it tonight. Please choose a mask and go on in. You're the first to arrive, so you'll have the dance floor to yourselves until the others arrive. Be sure to ask the band to play you a slow, jazzy tune."

Elizabeth and Reed chose masks and disappeared into the Trianon Suite, with matching smiles of anticipation on their faces.

Alex dragged a fingertip down Amanda's spine, whipping up waves of want. She loved it when he did that and every single time it made her hot. "We should have had a slow dance before our guests arrived."

Amanda looked into his eyes and the desire she saw made her breath catch. How could he look at her like that if he wanted that Chelsea woman? Maybe he'd told the truth about his relationship with the redhead. She hoped so. "Maybe we can have a dance after everyone leaves."

"I'm not waiting until the end of the night to hold you."

The determination in his low-voiced statement made her stomach flip and her pulse flutter. "I don't want you to."

More fool her. This was going to be a *big* relationship train wreck if she didn't find a way to pull back emotionally. But a tiny part of her wanted to savor every moment just in case. Just in case disaster struck and she found herself pregnant.

Ellen and Harry Harper arrived next. Amanda smiled. She enjoyed Alex's parents' company, and she hoped the night wasn't too hectic for her to find time to talk to them. But she couldn't help but be curious about the mystery surrounding Zack's parenthood. If Ellen hadn't had an affair, then what was the secret worth a million dollars?

Alex's hand settled on Amanda's waist—a circumstance his parents didn't miss. Ellen beamed and Harry nodded. But they'd barely exchanged hellos before another group of guests arrived.

Amanda spent the next two hours in a hypervigilant state as Alex's hostess. Even when he left her side it was as if some internal radar made her aware of his location, and it annoyed her that she couldn't seem to turn the Alex-detection system off. Each time their eyes met across the room her heart hiccuped.

She really had it bad for him and that wasn't good.

"Hey, you. How's it going?" Julia waltzed up beside her, accompanied by Elizabeth Wellington.

"Great. The Mardi Gras theme seems to be a big hit with Alex's employees. The incognito factor relaxes people, and everyone's having a good time if the number of smiles I see beneath the half masks are any indication."

"You always throw a great party, Amanda," Elizabeth said.

"Please feel free to shout that from the rooftop anytime, Elizabeth. Better yet, take out an ad in the *Times*." She winked at the women. "Where are your men?"

Julia dipped her head to indicate an area on the far side of the room. Amanda followed her gaze. Max and Reed had joined Senator Kendrick and the mayor. All the men's expressions were intense, as if they were cooking up a business deal.

"It's always sad when a marriage ends," Elizabeth said. "I read in the gossip section of the paper that the senator and Charmaine, his wife of thirty years, are divorcing." The tinge of pain in Elizabeth's voice hinted at the difficulties she and Reed had been through. "Not too long ago I thought Reed and I were headed down that painful path."

Amanda nodded. She'd noticed the tension while planning the Wellingtons' event. "I'm glad you managed to work out your issues. It's depressing when any relationship ends. They all leave scars—even if ending them is the best option available."

And she had the history to prove it.

Gage Lattimer, Reed Wellington's business partner and the occupant of the other 721 Park penthouse, joined the men. Usually Gage was a loner, but tonight Amanda had seen him working the crowd. He appeared to be having a good time.

"Gage has been a social butterfly tonight. He looks quite cheerful for a change. Do you think something or *someone* has gotten into him? It would be great if he'd settle down."

Julia's expression turned curious. "He had a bitter

divorce years ago. It'll take him awhile to put that behind him. Max claims Gage came away from the bitchy ex with a really hard shell. Good luck to the woman who tries to crack it."

Julia handed her plate to a passing waiter. "I want another dance with my husband before I go home and crash. Pregnancy is exhausting. I've never had so many early nights."

"That sounds like a wonderful idea," Elizabeth seconded. "Again, a lovely party, Amanda."

The women left Amanda alone. Moments later a tap on her elbow caught her attention. Alex's father and mother stood beside her.

"You're good for my son, Amanda," Harry announced. "I've never seen Alex look happier."

Amanda's gaze jerked across the room and slammed into Alex's heated regard. Her breath stalled and her insides warmed at the desire he made no effort to conceal. How unlike Alex to come out of his conservative shell and reveal his hunger in a public forum.

"I hope this means we'll see a lot more of you in the future." Harry's voice pulled her attention back to him.

"You'll definitely see more of me as we plan Zack's birthday party."

And they'd see a lot of her if she was carrying their grandchild.

She still hoped she wasn't.

It would be different if Alex loved her. Then the bad timing and the fear of being as lousy a parent as hers had been wouldn't be as anxiety-inducing. With his assistance she'd be able to hire help so she wouldn't have to neglect Affairs by Amanda, and her bad parenting examples would be counteracted by Alex's great ones. She truly envied him and Zack their parents.

Ellen stiffened and paled. Amanda followed her gaze to the entrance of the ballroom. The redhead from Alex's office stood poised in the doorway in a drop-dead, gorgeous, black form-fitting, cleavage-revealing dress.

Amanda's stomach pitched as if she'd gone over the top of a roller coaster. What was the woman doing here? There hadn't been any Chelseas on the guest list and because of the space limitations this was an invitation-only event.

What could she possibly want? Or maybe the question was *Who?* Amanda couldn't decide whether to ask Alex if he'd privately invited the newcomer or just insist the woman leave.

"Excuse me," Harry said and then stalked toward the interloper. His long, purposeful stride reminded her of Alex's. So maybe the son had inherited a characteristic from his father after all. Ellen stayed beside Amanda, but the smile she'd been wearing seconds ago had turned brittle.

Amanda glanced back at Alex to see if he'd noted Chelsea's arrival, but he was still deeply engrossed in a conversation with the senator.

Mr. Harper hustled Chelsea to an anteroom. Seconds later Amanda heard raised voices. They weren't loud enough to make out the words, but the argument drew the guests' attention—and Alex's. Amanda hurried across the ballroom to ask them to quiet down. Before she arrived the door opened and Mr. Harper escorted the redhead out. Twin dots of angry color marred Chelsea's beautiful face. Amanda felt no sympathy for her.

Harry didn't pause as he passed. "Good night, Amanda."

Alex's mother followed them out of the ballroom.

Amanda stared after them. What had that been about?

She searched for Alex and found him still with the senator, but he was tense, tight-lipped and definitely not looking like the happy host at the moment.

She'd have to intervene if she wanted to save the situation. But one thing was certain. That woman had put a damper on the event and Amanda wasn't going to rest until she found out why and what power Chelsea held over the Harper family, Alex in particular.

Ten

The new, unsmiling Alex of the past hour had surprised and confused Amanda. The only thing that shocked her more was when he dropped her off at her apartment door and turned away without kissing her good-night or asking to come in.

Let him go, she told herself as she studied his stiff back. But she couldn't. He was upset and she needed to know why and to help him with the issue if she could.

"Alex?" He paused in the hall, but didn't face her. "What's going on? Chelsea's appearance at the party cast a pall over the remainder of the evening—and not just because she wasn't on the guest list. She upset your parents and you."

After several seconds he turned to face her, one clearly reluctant but deliberate step at a time. His jaw looked rigid, as if he had his teeth clenched. "Inside."

He followed her into the apartment and closed the door but didn't sit. Instead he walked the strip of hardwood floor between the front door and the bedroom hallway and back again. Amanda waited, her own tension increasing as the seconds ticked past. She'd bet he looked very much like this when he was in court. Cool. Composed. Determined.

He stopped in front of her. "Chelsea reappears in my life every few years, usually when she needs money. This time she's calling her demand an 'investment opportunity' in some artist her gallery represents."

He thought Chelsea only wanted money? He couldn't possibly be so naive, could he? "Did she send the blackmail note?"

His eyes narrowed. "That's an astute question. One I've asked myself. But after talking to her neither the police nor I believe so."

"Then why did her presence tonight upset everyone? And why would she keep coming back for more money and expecting to get it?"

He took a deep breath and loosened his tie. The fabric whistled through his collar as he ripped it free and then stuffed it in his pocket. Next he removed his coat and tossed it over the back of a chair. His usual smooth moves were jerky and abrupt as if tightly leashed anger drove each action.

"Chelsea is Zack's mother."

Amanda gasped in surprise.

"And I'm Zack's father."

Her knees buckled. Head reeling, she sank onto the sofa. She hadn't seen that coming. But it explained so much, like the closeness between the "brothers" and the times she'd caught Alex studying Zack as if he were searching for something or soaking up details. "Oh, Alex."

"Chelsea has never been a part of Zack's life and couldn't care less about him. She's never even met her son and doesn't want to meet him now."

"How could she do that? He's an amazing young man. Smart and funny and sweet."

"I agree."

Amanda did some mental math. The numbers weren't good. "You were very young when she got pregnant."

"Barely seventeen. I wasn't ready to be a father. For a number of reasons I didn't believe the baby was mine, and I offered to pay for an abortion. By then I'd learned enough about Chelsea to know she'd make all of us miserable. I wasn't willing to marry her."

Amanda decided her possible pregnancy was not something she needed to spring on him now. Dread curled in her stomach.

"Chelsea went behind my back to my parents and threatened to not only make a public fuss about her pregnancy but to terminate if they didn't cough up a million dollars. My parents were horrified, both by the possible scandal that could have irrevocably damaged my father's reputation and by the idea of losing their first grandchild.

"Instead of letting Chelsea end the pregnancy they not only paid her the money she demanded, they decided to adopt Zack. My mother had always wanted more children but couldn't have them. She claimed Zack was her second chance."

Typical of a man, Alex had focused on the facts and not the emotions wrapped up in the events. "How did you feel about that?"

"What I wanted didn't matter. I was powerless. Completely and totally powerless." The anger and frustration in his voice said more than his words. It didn't bode well for her situation. If there was a situation.

His frustration also explained why he was such a workaholic now. He wanted the power he'd been denied back then.

"Mom cooked up an elaborate scheme. She and Chelsea moved to Paris until after Zack was born. As soon as a paternity test confirmed Zack was mine, my parents started the adoption procedure. My father visited Paris often enough during the pregnancy so that when my mother returned with a newborn, no one doubted that Zack was my father's child."

"And it helped because he looks just like you."

He inclined his head. "You mentioned that before. That's why I suspected you of the extortion note. You and my mother hit it off so well I was afraid she'd let something slip and you'd decided to capitalize on the information."

"She did let something slip, but I misinterpreted it. You don't think I'm capable of extortion now?"

He shook his head. "I haven't since we first discussed it."

She should take comfort in that, she supposed. "And you've told no one else about Zack's parentage?"

"Never. Not even Max knows."

But Alex had trusted her. The knowledge warmed her. "Then who could be behind the note?"

"I don't know. But I must find out before Zack is hurt."

The shock would be hard on the teen. "You should tell him, Alex."

"You're the second person to suggest that. I don't agree. Right now Zack trusts me. He's going through a rough spell, and he comes to me with problems he won't discuss with anyone else. If I tell him I abandoned him, I'll blow that trust."

"You didn't abandon him."

He fisted his hands by his side. "I didn't live up to my responsibility as his father. I took the easy way out and let my parents pay for my mistake. Hell, I didn't even want him to be born. When I think about not having him in my life and what I would have missed if Chelsea had done as I asked—" His voice cracked.

She fell a little deeper in love with him at that moment. Alex would be a wonderful father. But given his history with Chelsea, Amanda wasn't sure they would have even a slight chance at a healthy relationship if she turned up pregnant.

Chelsea had trapped him and used him and she'd taken his money. Amanda had used Alex for his connections and accepted a loan from him. She hadn't trapped him. Yet. And she didn't want to. But two black marks out of three didn't look good.

"Alex, you were little more than a child yourself."

"It doesn't matter. I wasn't there for Zack."

"I think you're wrong. I think you have been there for him from the moment you made the decision to relinquish him. I've seen the closeness between you. That doesn't develop without a lot of love and trust. But if you don't tell him and he finds out from someone else, his sense of betrayal will only be worse. You and your parents should sit down with him."

"I want him to know. I've wanted to tell him for years. But I don't want to lose him." The agony on his face revealed how much he struggled with the dilemma and responsibility. "Everyone he loves and trusts, me and our parents, have been living a lie."

She rose and crossed the room to wrap her arms around him. A hug wasn't much, but she'd craved them often enough and done without while growing up to want to offer the comfort the simple gesture provided.

Alex's arms banded around her so tightly she could barely draw a breath. She leaned back to look into his eyes. "What can I do to help?"

He pulled her close again and kissed her temple. "I wish I knew. I feel as if I have a live bomb in my hand. Someone has set the timer, but I can't read it. I have no idea how much time I have left before it blows everything to hell and back."

He'd feel even worse when he learned her secret. The only thing she could do was try to prove she loved him with actions, not words, and then if Murphy's Law did strike and she turned up pregnant maybe he'd trust her to do the right thing for their baby and for them.

That staggering thought took her aback when she realized she was actually considering having Alex Harper's baby and trying to build a family with him.

With her relationship track record that wasn't just risky. It was a potential catastrophe on a grand scale. But some chances were worth taking.

Amanda cupped Alex's tense jaw. It was late. Well past midnight. But she couldn't wait. "Make love with me, Alex."

And it would be love. For the first time in her life she would be truly making love. Not just having sex. Not just suffering from infatuation. She realized now that what she'd felt for Heath, Douglas and Curtis had been nothing more than blind infatuation.

What she felt for Alex was the kind of emotion musi-
cians, novelists and poets wrote about, the kind that filled
her with anticipation, excitement and fear.

Especially fear. But that fear gave life an exhilarating
edge. This could go so badly. Or it could be wonderful.
She intended to shoot for wonderful.

Alex turned his face into her touch and covered the back
of her hand with his. He planted a kiss in the heart of her
palm. His lips trailed to her wrist and any lingering tired-
ness she might have had from her day of hustling vanished.

His mouth burned a trail to the inside of her elbow, up
to her shoulder, then to the side of her neck. Amanda tilted
her head to the side to grant him better access. She adored
the way he nuzzled her neck, creating a swirl of desire in
her belly. His other hand cupped her waist, holding her
close while he sipped and nipped his way from her neck
along her jaw to her mouth.

She leaned into him, savoring the strength of his hips
and thighs. His tongue sought hers, stroked and swirled,
carrying her into a maelstrom of need. One big hand
caressed her back. The other splayed over her bottom
and pressed her against his growing erection. She shifted
against him and his breath hissed.

She needed to touch him. All of him. To absorb as
much of him into her being as she possibly could. His
scent. His taste. His heat. Amanda reached for the buttons
of his shirt and quickly freed them. His chest was firm
and hot beneath her hands. His tiny nipple beaded under
her tongue. She rapidly dealt with his belt and zipper and
impatiently shoved his clothing to the floor.

Alex kicked off his shoes. Amanda marched him
backward until the back of his legs hit the sofa. She shoved

and he sat. She knelt before him and peeled off his black socks. Pressing his knees apart, she made a place for herself between them. His thick shaft stood tall and tempting in front of her. Her mouth watered, and her inner thighs warmed and wanted. She licked her lips, but as much as she needed him inside her, she had a better idea.

He wasn't ready to hear the words, but she'd show him how much she loved him, beginning with a foot massage. She captured one big foot and dug her thumbs into his sole. Alex groaned and leaned against the cushions. She kissed the arch of his foot while her fingers plied his flesh, and then she painted a circle around his ankle bone with her tongue.

She repeated the process with his other foot and then, working her way up from his foot, she massaged his calf and up his thigh. Her lips trailed close behind. Inside his knee. Up his inner thigh. His muscles grew tenser with each inch her hands and mouth climbed. The dark hairs on his legs tickled her lips and skin. She licked the tender sac beneath his penis.

"Amanda," Alex growled, but he didn't stop her explorations or protest when she drew intricate patterns with her tongue.

She licked the length of his rigid flesh and his fingers speared into her hair. He cradled her head gently, but his hands trembled. She found the swollen head of his arousal and took him into her mouth. She tasted, sucked and stroked, pleased that she could make him quiver the way he did her.

She loved him with her mouth, caressed him with her hands. His breath whooshed out in a half groan. His knees clamped on his shoulders and his legs clenched. She savored the harsh rasp of his breathing, the spasm of his fingers in her hair. His hips flexed and then he clamped down on her head and pulled her away.

"I wasn't finished," she protested.

"Neither am I," he rasped as he stood, cupping her elbows and pulling her to her feet with him. He quickly removed her clothing, and then he swept her into his arms and laid her on the sofa.

One hard kiss pressed her head against the cushion. A second branded her left breast. He drew her nipple deep into his mouth, rolled it with his tongue and razed it gently with his teeth. His hand found the other, plucking, teasing it.

Her middle melted like paraffin wax. She bit her lip on a moan and arched her back. Alex traced a line down the center of her belly with his fingers. He delved into her curls and found her slickness. Using her own moisture, he fondled, caressed, buffed her sensitive center and then plunged his fingers deep inside her. Hunger rolled through her. Her knees opened involuntarily to give him better access and her heels dug into the sofa, lifting her into his touch.

He shamelessly took advantage. She squeezed him with her internal muscles, silently begging for more. His tempo quickened, rushing her to a rapid ascent and then sending her crashing over. One release followed another without giving her time to catch her breath until, weak and gasping, she covered the hand buried in her curls.

"Alex, I need you." She cupped his nape and pulled him forward. He took her mouth in a kiss so deep and carnal and on the edge of control it stopped just shy of painful.

With a groan he disconnected, grabbed his pants,

fished in his pocket and found a condom which he quickly applied. Alex looked like a man on a mission. Determination hardened his jaw. Passion blazed in his eyes.

She wanted to slow him down, to savor making love for the first time while being in love. "Wait."

He paused, each muscle bunched and quivering.

"I want to be on top."

His eyes closed. His head fell back. He sucked a deep breath through his nose and then lay back on the sofa. Amanda climbed over him, straddled him and without taking her eyes off his face, eased down to take him into her body, into her heart, into her soul.

She loved this man. He stretched her, filled her, completed her. In all of her wild and crazy, detour-ridden life, this was the only time she'd ever been absolutely certain she was exactly where she was supposed to be and with whom she was destined to be.

No matter what happened from here on out, Alex would always be a part of her life. He'd left his mark on her. And baby or no baby, she would never forget him and never, ever be free of his memory.

She needed to find a way to make him feel the same.

"Amanda?" Alex called out Sunday morning from Amanda's shower. "I need soap."

Silence greeted him and he remembered her mentioning as she climbed out of bed while he'd been still half-asleep that she wanted to dash out to Park Café for a couple of her favorite chocolate muffins. A smile tugged his lips. She had a thing for those muffins.

And he had a thing for her. More than a thing, he decided as the hot water beat down on his back.

He'd fallen in love with her.

Love. Not an emotion he'd ever expected to experience.

But he and Amanda were a damned good team. Her understanding last night had put the final nail in the coffin of his determination to remain single. She was good with Zack, got along with his parents, drove him wild in bed and was an asset to his career. Look how she'd salvaged the evening last night after Chelsea's appearance had turned his mood sour. If not for Amanda he would have blown the alliance he'd made with the senator and killed the party spirit for his employees.

And then there was the way she'd tackled him on the sofa after they returned to her place. His grin turned salacious and his blood simmered. He'd need a cold shower before she returned if he kept up that line of thought, or she wouldn't get to eat her muffins before the chocolate chips cooled.

He wasn't going to let her go.

The realization sobered him. Keeping her meant marriage. He'd never planned to marry, never planned to trust another woman not to screw him over. But he'd tie himself to Amanda in a heartbeat. He loved and trusted her.

"Amanda?" he called out again. He wanted to tell her how he felt.

On second thought, not yet. He had to come up with something big, a grand gesture a woman who planned events for a living would appreciate. And he had to buy a ring. Maybe Zack could help him choose one.

Alex eyed the tiny, almost transparent sliver of soap in his hand. It wasn't going to get the job done and if Amanda wasn't here he'd have to find a new bar himself.

He pulled back the shower curtain and stepped onto the lavender bathmat. Steam slowly filled the room from the hot water running behind him as he knelt to open the vanity cabinet and scan the contents. No soap. He shifted lotions, tampons, shampoo, a leg-waxing kit and a jumble of other woman products. This was why he didn't cohabitate. Women had too much junk cluttering up the space. Good thing his bathroom in Greenwich was large enough to accommodate all of Amanda's paraphernalia.

He didn't see what he needed, but a bag in the back of the cabinet snagged his attention. He made out the shape of a rectangle through the plastic. Soap? He snagged the handle, opened the top and looked inside.

A pregnancy test.

The hairs on the back of his neck prickled. He dismissed the reaction and started to shove the bag back where he'd found it. Julia had probably left the item behind. But the corner of the receipt tucked inside the bag caught his eye. Checking the date to confirm his suspicions wouldn't hurt. He grabbed the corner, yanked out the white strip and scanned the print.

An Arctic chill swept through him when he saw the date.

The test kit had been purchased four days ago. *Four days.* It wasn't Julia's.

Why would Amanda need a pregnancy test?

Denial screamed through him and a sense of déjà vu seized him by the throat. Amanda wouldn't plot to take him to the cleaners the way Chelsea had.

Or would she?

Hadn't every woman he'd become involved with over the years eventually pulled some kind of manipulative crap to keep the relationship going long after the embers had cooled?

Amanda was short on cash and she'd been tense lately. Had she cultivated the friendship with his parents to use them against him? If so, she'd learn he wasn't a powerless teen who ran from his responsibilities anymore.

He heard the front door open, stood and whipped a towel around his hips. After turning off the water, he grabbed the kit and stormed out to meet her.

Amanda saw him and stopped. A slow, wicked smile slid across her lips and her gaze glided over his face and bare chest, skidding to a halt on the box in his hand.

Her eyes widened and her lips parted. Her shocked gaze locked with his. Color flooded her cheeks—guilty color—and then leeched away to leave her ghostly pale.

"When were you going to tell me?" he forced himself to say.

"I—I—I don't know if I am yet. I haven't taken the test. There's nothing to tell."

He'd wanted her to deny it and when she didn't, his muscles tensed even more. "How late are you?"

She blinked and swallowed twice the way a witness did when buying time. "Only a few days."

"Is it mine?"

She flinched. "If I am pregnant, then yes, it's yours. I haven't been with anyone else in a long time."

Fury boiled inside him along with betrayal. "Did you set me up?"

Her eyes widened even farther and then anger stormed her face. She strode into the room, the Park Café bag clutched in one hand. She dropped it on the coffee table. "Set you up? Do you think I want to be pregnant?"

"You wouldn't be the first woman to see me as a ticket to Easy Street."

"I'm not Chelsea. And it took two of us to create this situation. You didn't wear a condom that first time."

He searched his mind for details and recalled he'd been so eager and impatient to have her that night he'd taken her standing up. Damnation. That was exactly the kind of idiot mistake he always warned Zack not to make.

"If there is a child I want joint custody."

She closed her eyes tightly, inhaled, exhaled, then lifted her lids. Worry darkened her grey eyes to almost charcoal. "Let's not panic prematurely. We don't know if there is a baby yet."

"That's easy enough to find out." He thrust the box toward her. "Take the test."

Looking horrified, she staggered back a step and the box fell to the sofa. "Alex—"

"Do it now."

The door buzzer sounded. Amanda startled and then looked relieved by the interruption. She hurried to the intercom. "Yes?"

"A Zack Harper is here to see you," the doorman's voice said.

Zack? Uneasiness crept up Alex's spine. Why would Zack track him down unless something was wrong?

"Send him up," Amanda instructed and then turned back to Alex. "Why would Zack come to my place and so early on a Sunday morning?" She stashed the pregnancy test behind an oversize pillow on the sofa.

"My thoughts exactly."

"Alex, you might want to get dressed."

Right. He hustled to Amanda's room and jerked on his

tux pants and shirt. He didn't have anything else to wear.
A knock at the door had him hurrying back to the living
room barefooted.

Zack looked like hell. His hair was disheveled, his
face drawn with fatigue.

Amanda rested a hand on his shoulder. "Are you okay?"

Zack looked up and spotted Alex. "Tell me it's not true."

The pain in Zack's voice ripped into Alex like a knife.
He knew. Somehow Zack had discovered the truth.

"Tell me you're not my father." He confirmed Alex's
worst fear.

A heavy weight settled on his chest. "I can't do that,
Zack."

"Why? Why did you lie?" Zack shouted.

His obvious pain twisted the knife in Alex's gut. "How
did you find out?"

"Does it matter? You lied to me."

Amanda wrapped her arm around Zack's tense shoulders, pulled him into the apartment and closed the door.
"Zack, Alex had good reasons for making the decisions
he did. And you need to hear them."

Amanda's support surprised Alex, especially given
what he'd just accused her of doing.

She led Zack to the sofa and sat beside him. "Tell us
how you found out."

"Mom and Dad were arguing last night about some
woman wanting money. My *mother*—" His voice broke.
Amanda took one of his fists in hers and slowly un-
clenched his fingers to hold his hand in both of hers.
"They said as long as she knew who my real father was
she would keep coming back for more money. She's
bribing them."

Alex realized Amanda and the detective were right. He should have told Zack the truth sooner. It was always better to avert a crisis than to clean up after one.

It was time to come clean. "I was your age when I got Chelsea pregnant. I was young and selfish and I wasn't ready to be a father."

Zack inhaled sharply. "You wanted to get rid of me?"

Lying would be the kindest thing to do. But he'd lied for too long already. "I thought my life would be over if I had a child. No college. No friends. Yes, I tried to convince Chelsea to terminate. She went to my—*our*—parents instead. They wanted to adopt you and made plans to do so. It was the best decision anyone could have made, Zack. But I was too young and too stupid to know that at the time. And I was very fortunate to have been allowed to watch you grow up and be a part of your life. I don't regret one second of that."

"Why didn't you tell me?" Anger and hurt still filled Zack's voice and his eyes.

"I didn't want to hurt or confuse you. But I've done that anyway. I'm sorry."

"Zack." Amanda waited until Zack looked at her. "You're dating now. How would you feel if one of your girlfriends turned up pregnant?"

Zack jerked. "Rotten…scared. Angry."

"And maybe a little bit trapped and panicked? You'd worry about not being able to do all the things you'd wanted to do, wouldn't you? You're excited about going to college at Harry and Alex's alma mater, aren't you? But you'd have a baby coming about the same time all of your friends would be packing their bags and heading for orientation. They'd be leaving you behind."

The frown on Zack's face deepened. "Yeah."

Amanda squeezed his hand. "Unless you decided not to become a father. That's what Alex faced. He was in a tough spot. Making difficult choices is part of life. Making mistakes is human. We all do it. Fixing them, owning up to them and making the best out of a bad situation are signs of maturity. Listen to Alex. Let him explain his side of the story. He's a pretty great guy. But I think you already know that."

Amanda rose. "I need to take my shower. I'll leave you to talk."

Alex watched her walk out of the room. Why had she stood by him after he'd treated her like crap?

Because that's the kind of person Amanda Crawford was. And he'd blown it.

He turned to Zack. He saw the pain and confusion in the eyes so like his own. His throat burned and his heart ached for the pain he'd caused Zack. He crossed to take Amanda's place on the couch.

"I'm sorry, Zack. I've wanted to tell you for years. I probably should have. But I was afraid I'd screw up the bond between us. I'm proud of you, Zack. You've turned into one hell of a great kid. And I'd like to think that I've been a part of that even if I couldn't be your father."

Tears filled Zack's eyes. He blinked them away. "I wish you'd told me."

"Would it have made a difference? We have amazing parents. We couldn't do better."

"But you're my father."

"Biologically, yes. In my heart, absolutely. But otherwise, no. Harry Harper is your father—*our* father—in every way that counts."

And it damn near killed him to admit that. All these years he'd believed he could have been a good parent if the power hadn't been taken from him, but he finally had to admit he'd never be a better father than his had been. And it had nothing to do with power and everything to do with being there.

"Do the folks know where you are?"

Zack shifted uncomfortably and looked away. "No. I spent the night at your house. I tried to call your cell phone. You didn't answer. I used my key and let myself in. But you didn't come home."

"As you've guessed, I stayed with Amanda. But then you always were a smart kid." Alex snagged his tux jacket from the back of the chair and retrieved his cell phone from his pocket. He checked for missed calls and found ten of them, some from his parents, some from Zack. He'd never heard it ring. "I had it on vibrate and I left my jacket in here last night."

"Did you love her?"

Alex stiffened. He'd barely admitted his feelings for Amanda to himself. Was he ready to share them with Zack? No. And did her hiding her possible pregnancy from him change how he felt? Yes. No. He had no clue.

But Zack had used past tense. "Did I love who?"

"My mother. My *birth* mother."

Alex shoved a hand through his hair and expelled a relieved breath. Zack wasn't talking about Amanda. *Tell the truth.* "No. We were just two kids screwing around and we got caught."

"That's why you always harp about safe sex."

"I don't harp."

"Yes, you do. Repeatedly. Jeez, you even bought me condoms before I kissed a girl the first time."

Alex grimaced. So maybe he'd been a little overzealous. "You're the best thing that's ever happened to me, Zack. Don't ever doubt that. And when I think about what could have happened…"

"But it didn't. What is it Amanda always says? Everything happens for a reason and we each have to find our path even if it isn't the beaten one?"

"Amanda says that?"

Amanda said a lot of things. Things that should have clued him in to the fact that she was nothing like Chelsea. She hadn't set him up. Her patching it up between him and Zack was a perfect example of Amanda's priorities.

He'd falsely accused her. Twice. First for sending the extortion note, and second for trying to trap him. Amanda was all about people. Their feelings. Their hearts. Not their bank balances. She would never do anything to deliberately hurt someone. His lack of trust could very well cost him the best woman he'd ever known.

"I like her. You should keep her." Zack reached for the muffin bag Amanda had dropped on the coffee table. The kid was a bottomless pit where food was concerned.

Alex rested a hand on Zack's shoulder. "I intend to. And for that, I might need your help."

"You mean work as a team?" Zack shrugged. "Sure. I'm in. But only if you swear to tell me the whole truth from now on."

"I will."

"What do you need?"

"Forgiveness. I said some things to Amanda that she might not be willing to forgive or forget."

"I'll put in a good word for you, but Amanda isn't the type to hold grudges."

Alex laughed. How could a kid half his age be wiser than him about women? "I hope you're right."

Because if Amanda wouldn't forgive him he wasn't sure what he'd do. One thing was certain. He wasn't giving her up without a fight.

Eleven

Amanda Crawford, you're a hypocrite.

Amanda stood in her bedroom listening to the low hum of Alex's and Zack's conversation and scolded herself. How could she preach about owning up to mistakes when she wasn't willing to face or admit hers?

First thing Monday morning she'd call Alex's associate and sic him on Curtis. It might be embarrassing initially, but in the long run it was the right thing to do. If she didn't stop Curtis, what was to keep him from doing to someone else what he'd already done to her?

And she needed to take the pregnancy test...but it was in the living room. She wasn't going to tromp in there and interrupt their conversation to fetch it. The last thing Zack needed was to have the bomb dropped on him that he might be a real brother soon.

She'd do the test as soon as she returned from visiting her parents.

But before she could take those giant steps, she needed to call her parents and come clean. Pleasing them was an impossible task. She needed to quit wasting her time on the effort. From now on she had to live her life and find her path to happiness. She'd said that often enough to others. It was time she took her own advice. And if her parents couldn't handle that she was human and made mistakes, then tough.

Alex had no idea how lucky he was to have parents who supported him no matter how big his blunder. She hoped her parents would learn to accept her decisions—the good ones *and* the bad ones—one of these days. If they chose not to, then missing out on their grandchild—if there was one— would be their loss. She wouldn't expose any child of hers to the bitter negativity she'd endured while growing up.

Before she could chicken out she picked up the phone and punched in her parents' number. Her mother answered.

"Hi, Mom. I need to talk to you and Daddy. Today."

"Amanda, we're booked for couples tennis with—"

"Mother, make time for me or read about what I'm going to tell you in the paper."

Silence stretched through the airwaves. "Be here within the hour."

"I'm on my way."

Amanda disconnected and headed for the door. She didn't put on makeup or change her clothes. Her mother would have a lot to say about that. But who cared?

This visit was all about acceptance. It was time her parents realized she was her own person and she had no desire to be a little clone of either of them.

Alex and Zack looked up as she entered the living room. "I'm going out. Lock up when you leave."

Before they could respond, she tossed Alex her spare key, stepped into the hall and closed the door. He didn't need the key to secure the apartment. Giving him one was symbolic of her willingness to let him into her life. Would he get the message?

As soon as she dealt with her parental issues, she'd have to return and deal with the much larger issue of Alex…and the pregnancy test.

But she could jump only one hurdle at a time, and she wasn't sure which item on the agenda scared her the most. Opening her heart to Alex or taking the test. Funny, it wasn't facing her parents' disapproval. A week ago it would have been.

A quick cab ride dumped her at her parents' apartment on Fifth Avenue. The housekeeper let her in—another new one, she noticed. Because Dominique Crawford was demanding and impossible to please, staff turnover was frequent. Amanda had learned long ago to never get attached to Crawford employees. They never lasted long.

She found her parents in the morning room, gathering their belongings to leave even though they'd known she was coming.

"You need to sit down and listen instead of acting like I'm the least important part of your life and you'd rather be elsewhere."

Amanda watched her mother's eyebrows rise and then turned to her father. He laid his tennis racket on the glass-topped table and resumed his seat. "Your rudeness does not impress me, Amanda."

She bit down on the urge to apologize. It was way past

time for her to stand up to them, and she was through apologizing to them for not being the daughter they'd wanted. It was time they accepted her, warts and all, instead of trying to mold her into something else.

"In the next few months the Crawford name might make it into the papers." She ignored their disapproving scowls and continued. "I ended my affair with Curtis Wilks not because he dumped me like I told you, but because he had embezzled from Affairs by Amanda. I was too embarrassed up until now to admit that or to pursue legal action against him. Tomorrow that changes. I'm going to call an associate of Alex Harper's."

"Amanda, another escapade? Honestly, how do you keep finding trouble?" Her mother's questions raised Amanda's hackles.

"Is a public scandal necessary? You'll cost your mother and me credibility."

"Daddy, I have to do what's right for me, and for once I'd like your support instead of your fault-finding."

Dominique stiffened. "We don't—"

"You do. You refuse to accept that I'm not interested in fashion, and Daddy hates the fact that I'd rather pluck out my eyelashes one by one than read ticker tape all day. Why can't you just accept that I'm good at what I do? Affairs by Amanda is growing steadily every year. I love my job and I'm a success, just not in your chosen fields."

While her parents silently digested her statements, she gathered her courage to lay the big news on them.

"There are a couple of other things you need to know. One, I've fallen in love with Alex Harper."

"That's wonderful," her mother replied with a blinding smile. No surprise there. Amanda had known they'd approve of Alex given his income, lineage, occupation and address.

"Don't get excited. Something has happened to make him distrust me…and there's no guarantee we'll have a future together." She took a deep breath. "I might be pregnant with his baby. And he thinks I got that way deliberately."

Shocked silence greeted her.

"If he won't marry you, you'll terminate, of course," her mother pronounced.

"No, Mother, I won't." She paused to silently reaffirm the decision she'd made in the taxi on the way over here. "I've decided that if I'm pregnant I'm keeping this baby. I want this small part of Alex. I know it won't be easy to be a single parent. But I won't tie Alex to me against his will by trying to force him to marry me. It isn't the right thing to do."

"Do you realize how badly a bastard grandchild will reflect on me?" her father groused.

"I'm sorry if you feel that way, Daddy, but this is not a business decision. This is a personal one. And we no longer live in the Dark Ages. Nearly forty percent of births these days are to unmarried mothers. It doesn't carry the stigma it used to."

Her mother gave a snooty sniff. "That's what people say to your face. Behind your back they say something else entirely. How soon will you know if you are?"

She wasn't going to call them the moment she had the test results. She'd need time to digest them, whatever they were. "Tomorrow morning."

"We want to know immediately," her mother said.

"You'll find out after I tell Alex. He and I are the ones

that matter most in this. Your support would be nice, but you've taught me I can live without it."

And that, she realized, was the lesson she was meant to learn from this experience. She didn't need her parents' approval to live her life.

It was funny how life never delivered the lessons until you needed them most.

A seductive smile replaced the surprise on Chelsea's face seconds after she opened her door to Alex later that Sunday.

"Alex, how wonderful to see you. Come in." She opened the door wider for him to enter. He didn't miss the calculating glint in her eyes. No doubt she was trying to figure out how much she could get out of him this time.

Even on a Sunday afternoon her makeup and clothing were flawless, and she didn't have a hair out of place— a far cry from Amanda, who had dashed out of her apartment this morning makeup-free and wearing jeans and an old Vassar sweatshirt. That didn't mean she hadn't looked mouthwateringly attractive, especially since he knew she never wore a bra under her sweatshirt.

Chelsea, on the other hand, was like Alex, always intense and prepared to close the next deal or wow the next client. Amanda was just Amanda. Relaxed, comfortable, easy to be with. She relied on her natural charm and her warm smile rather than props to win people over. She was someone he should have known he could take at face value without having to worry about ulterior motives behind her smile.

How could he have been blind to those qualities?

He followed Chelsea into her living room. Her cloying perfume filled his nose, making him wish for Amanda's pure scent, not heavy perfume. The difference between the women didn't stop there, he realized as he looked around Chelsea's showplace space and noted many of the pricey antiques she'd purchased, probably with his family's money. Chelsea was the epitome of a material girl. She had always believed in the adage "She who dies with the most valuables wins."

Amanda, on the other hand, had filled her apartment with colors and textures and treasures she'd bought not because of their resale value but because they'd caught her eye. She didn't dress herself or her home to impress others but to please her own taste.

She was genuine and honest, which made her keeping the secret about her late period out of character. The contradiction nagged at him. Why had she remained silent? And why hadn't he bothered to ask before she'd run out instead of just accusing her of having an ulterior motive?

By the time he'd taken Zack back to Greenwich and hashed the situation out with his parents, he hadn't been able to locate Amanda and she wasn't answering her cell phone.

"Did you reconsider making an investment in Auturo? Here's an example of his work." Chelsea gestured to a large abstract oil painting on the wall. It wasn't bad. But it wasn't great, either. He couldn't imagine Amanda liking the muted colors or lack of emotion in the piece. Was it a nude? Was it Chelsea? Could be. Chances were the artist was her latest live-in lover.

"I'm not interested in 'investing' in anything else with you ever again. Zack knows about us, Chelsea. You've lost the leverage to keep extorting money from me or my parents under whichever guise you choose to call it."

She inhaled quickly. "The blackmailer went to the press? Do they know I'm his mother?" She sounded horrified.

"No. But I will go public if necessary. Zack understands the situation and my family is willing to back whatever actions I deem necessary."

"But, Alex—"

"It's over, Chelsea. Don't contact me again unless you want to meet our son. But let me warn you, if you ever do anything to hurt him or make him uncomfortable I will come after you and tie you in so many legal knots you'll never get free. You've held the reins far too long and we've given you too much power. Rest assured, your actions have been well-documented, and you've left enough slack to hang yourself."

Worry tinged her eyes. "You wouldn't."

"You'll find that there's nothing I won't do for the ones I love. Zack. My parents. Amanda. Don't cross me."

He pivoted on his heel and stalked out of the apartment. One problem down. But the most important one loomed ahead.

He had to win Amanda back.

"Hello, Senator," Amanda said as she reached across the window table at the River Café in Brooklyn.

The senator stood and shook her hand. "So glad you could make it on short notice, Amanda."

"I'm happy to accommodate you. Your phone message mentioned an urgent party?"

Coming home to that message intrigued her. When added to an invitation for dinner at a place known for its delicious seafood and impressive view of New York Harbor and the Manhattan skyline, she couldn't say no.

The outing would provide a nice distraction from wondering where Alex was and how his meeting with Zack had gone, and worrying about that blasted pregnancy test that was still waiting for her and if Alex could forgive her for keeping her secret.

Yanking her thoughts back to the present, she took the seat the server held out for her. With her back to the door, she faced the gorgeous view.

Why would Michael Kendrick invite her to the restaurant voted most romantic in New York City? She surveyed the room again, this time with a professional eye. The space could easily hold anywhere from thirty to a hundred, depending on the type of party. She'd yet to use it as a venue, but she'd like to. But why was theirs the only occupied table? And why were there pedestals holding red rose bouquets in every corner? Surely the senator hadn't reserved the entire room for this meal?

A frisson of unease skipped down her nape. She knew he'd recently separated from his wife. Surely he didn't consider this a date? Not that he wasn't attractive, but he'd known her parents for years, and he was…well, old enough to be her father.

"Alex mentioned you were very good at short-notice events, and last night's party proves that statement." Kendrick sat back in his chair. "I have a very special occasion in mind. I'm told you are the only one equipped to handle the details."

A trickle of excitement wound through her. "Thank you for that vote of confidence. What kind of event?"

"I'd rather not say."

Strange. "It will be hard to plan without a few more details."

"We'll get to those momentarily."

She'd dealt with eccentric people before, but until now she hadn't considered the senator to be one of them. She'd thought him straightforward and conservative. But she could play along. She pulled her PDA from her purse. "As long as it's not illegal, I can work with you. What's your time frame?"

"That's where this gets a little bit tricky."

How could it get any trickier than planning an event for which she had no details?

"Excuse me a moment, Amanda, and I'll get that information for you." He rose and left her alone in the private dining room.

How odd. Had he left the data in his car?

Moments later she heard the senator's footsteps return. He reached his seat and she looked up from her calendar. But it wasn't Senator Kendrick standing across the table from her.

A grave, somber Alex looked down at her. Her pulse kicked erratically. He wore her favorite Brooks Brothers suit, charcoal grey with a subtle white pinstripe, a white shirt and a pink tie. Pink? Conservative Alex in pink? Pink might be her favorite color, but she'd never expected to see it on him. "Alex."

"Hello, Amanda." He lowered himself into the chair Kendrick had vacated.

"Where's the senator?"

"I wasn't sure you'd agree to meet me, so I asked Michael to help me out."

She frowned. "Why wouldn't I see you?"

"Because I unjustly accused you of trying to extort money from me and then of trying to trap me. Two strikes."

An unsteady breath shuddered into her lungs and back out again. "Yes, you did, and I won't deny it hurt. But after hearing what Chelsea has done I can understand how you might jump to the conclusion that I'd do the same. I did borrow money from you and use your connections. I have two strikes, too."

"You have no strikes with me. If anything, I owe you for showing me where I've gone wrong. I've been working insane hours trying to regain the power I lost when Chelsea became pregnant with Zack. I believed that being the top dog meant having all the control. But power is useless if the people you care about are not safe and happy."

His eyes searched hers. Keeping his hands in his lap, he sat straight and tense. This wasn't the charmer she'd come to know, the one who could talk her out of her clothes in record time.

"How did it go with Zack?"

"Not bad. We still have some issues to work out, but we should be fine, thanks to the way you explained the situation. As always, you managed to find exactly the right approach and say the right thing. You have a talent for reaching people on their level and for making them see what's important. You put him in my shoes. I would never have thought to do that."

His praise warmed her. "What's going on, Alex?"

"I need you to plan something for me."

She sighed. "You didn't need to go to all this trouble to offer me a job."

"It's a special event. A once-in-a-lifetime affair. Two of them, actually. And I'm giving you carte blanche."

Confused by the tension she read in him, she bit her lip. "I'm going to need a little more to go on than that."

"It's an engagement party followed by a wedding."

Her stomach did a queer little roll. She swallowed. "For whom?"

"Us."

Her heart skidded to a halt and then beat its way up her throat. "Us?"

He lifted one hand from his lap and covered hers on the table. "I've learned the hard way that women can rarely be trusted."

Ouch. She tried to pull away but his grip tightened around her wrist and held fast.

"Chelsea wasn't the only one to work me over for money or my connections."

Double ouch. But she had no idea where he was going with this so she didn't speak.

"I never planned to fall in love or get married."

What?

"And then I met you."

She couldn't make her lungs work.

"I've fallen in love with you, Amanda. Any way you look at it we're a damned good team. I want you in my life. Not temporarily. Permanently."

Those were the words she longed to hear, but... "This isn't because I'm late, is it? Because I might not be pregnant."

"This has nothing to do with that. But why haven't you taken the test? Don't you want to know?"

Good question. "I've been stalling because I wasn't sure how I'd handle the answer. I needed to weigh my options and decisions. And I wasn't sure how my parents would handle the news. But you know I finally figured out it doesn't matter what they think. This is *my* life. I get to live it *my* way. And if I make mistakes, it's okay because I'm living it instead of sitting safely on a fence and watching life pass me by.

"I was going to take the test as soon as I returned from my parents' this morning, but the senator's message said, 'Extremely urgent.' I had to dash right back out again."

"And you've made your decision?"

She took a deep breath and slowly exhaled. "Yes. If I'm pregnant, then I want to keep this baby."

He inhaled sharply.

"But, Alex, I would never use a child to tie you down or extort money from you. I have an inheritance from my grandparents coming soon. I won't need financial assistance. Yours or anyone else's."

"If you're carrying my baby then you'll get it anyway. And you'll have me by your side every step of the way. I'd like to raise children with you, Amanda."

The intensity of his voice made the hairs on her arms stand up. "If we got together now I'd always wonder whether it's because of an unplanned pregnancy."

"If we get together and we love each other, does it really matter how it happened?"

She flinched and warmth steamed her face. Had she been completely transparent? "I never said I loved you."

A lazy smile tilted his lips. "You've shown me with your actions, but I was too blind and distrustful to see that before now. I don't need words, but I wouldn't mind hearing them when you're ready."

Her heart pounded faster. "Alex—"

"I want you to plan the wedding of your dreams, Amanda. No limitations. No budget. Whatever you want, you can have it. As long as I'm the man waiting at the end of the aisle for you."

What he said sounded so good she was afraid to believe him. "That sounds like a bribe."

"Do I need to bribe you?" He reached into his coat pocket and then reached across the table. He opened his hand to reveal a blue Tiffany ring box.

Stunned speechless, she stared at the box. Hope fluttered to life in her chest.

"Marry me, Amanda, whether or not we've made a baby together." He lifted the lid to reveal an exquisite pear-shaped pink diamond flanked by two pale lavender tanzanite baguettes.

Pink. Her favorite color. Lavender, runner-up. And Alex hadn't had to ask. He'd taken the time to notice.

"Let me spend the rest of my life showing you how incredibly unique and special you are and why you're perfect."

"I'm far from perfect."

"You're perfect for me."

Her eyes stung and happiness swelled within her until she thought she'd burst with it. "I do love you, Alex."

He rose, came around the table. He took her hand, pulled her from her seat and into his arms. His lips brushed her forehead, her temple and finally her lips in a tender, lingering kiss. "Then say yes."

"Yes." How could she say anything else? Because as Alex had said, they were perfect for each other.

"Let's go home and take that test. After we make love."

She cupped his jaw in her hand, relishing his scent, his nearness, but mostly the love in his eyes. "And if making love takes all night?"

The naughty twinkle made her heart skip. "Then the

test will wait. Because we're going to be together regard-
less of the outcome."

Alex led her toward the door. Amanda couldn't keep the
smile off her face. For the second time, Alex had shown
her that she was right where she was supposed to be and
with whom she was destined to spend the rest of her life.

* * * * *

Here is a sneak preview of
A STONE CREEK CHRISTMAS,
the latest in Linda Lael Miller's acclaimed
McKETTRICK *series.*

A lonely horse brought vet Olivia O'Ballivan to
Tanner Quinn's farm, but it's the rancher's love that
might cause her to stay.

A STONE CREEK CHRISTMAS
Available December 2008
from Silhouette Special Edition

Tanner heard the rig roll in around sunset. Smiling, he wandered to the window. Watched as Olivia O'Ballivan climbed out of her Suburban, flung one defiant glance toward the house and started for the barn, the golden retriever trotting along behind her.

Taking his coat and hat down from the peg next to the back door, he put them on and went outside. He was used to being alone, even liked it, but keeping company with Doc O'Ballivan, bristly though she sometimes was, would provide a welcome diversion.

He gave her time to reach the horse Butterpie's stall, then walked into the barn.

The golden retriever came to greet him, all wagging tail and melting brown eyes, and he bent to stroke her soft, sturdy back. "Hey, there, dog," he said.

Sure enough, Olivia was in the stall, brushing Butterpie down and talking to her in a soft, soothing voice that touched something private inside Tanner and made him want to turn on one heel and beat it back to the house.

He'd be damned if he'd do it, though.

This was *his* ranch, *his* barn. Well-intentioned as she was, *Olivia* was the trespasser here, not him.

"She's still very upset," Olivia told him, without turning to look at him or slowing down with the brush.

Shiloh, always an easy horse to get along with, stood contentedly in his own stall, munching away on the feed Tanner had given him earlier. Butterpie, he noted, hadn't touched her supper as far as he could tell.

"Do you know anything at all about horses, Mr. Quinn?" Olivia asked.

He leaned against the stall door, the way he had the day before, and grinned. He'd practically been raised on horseback; he and Tessa had grown up on their grandmother's farm in the Texas hill country, after their folks divorced and went their separate ways, both of them too busy to bother with a couple of kids. "A few things," he said. "And I mean to call you Olivia, so you might as well return the favor and address me by my first name."

He watched as she took that in, dealt with it, decided on an approach. He'd have to wait and see what that turned out to be, but he didn't mind. It was a pleasure just watching Olivia O'Ballivan grooming a horse.

"All right, *Tanner*," she said. "This barn is a disgrace. When are you going to have the roof fixed? If it snows again, the hay will get wet and probably mold…"

He chuckled, shifted a little. He'd have a crew out there the following Monday morning to replace the roof and

shore up the walls—he'd made the arrangements over a
week before—but he felt no particular compunction to
explain that. He was enjoying her ire too much; it made
her color rise and her hair fly when she turned her head,
and the faster breathing made her perfect breasts go up and
down in an enticing rhythm. "What makes you so sure I'm
a greenhorn?" he asked mildly, still leaning on the gate.

At last she looked straight at him, but she didn't move
from Butterpie's side. "Your hat, your boots—that fancy
red truck you drive. I'll bet it's customized."

Tanner grinned. Adjusted his hat. "Are you telling me
real cowboys don't drive red trucks?"

"There are lots of trucks around here," she said. "Some
of them are red, and some of them are new. And *all* of
them are splattered with mud or manure or both."

"Maybe I ought to put in a car wash, then," he teased.
"Sounds like there's a market for one. Might be a good
investment."

She softened, though not significantly, and spared him
a cautious half smile, full of questions she probably
wouldn't ask. "There's a good car wash in Indian Rock,"
she informed him. "People go there. It's only forty miles."

"Oh," he said with just a hint of mockery. "*Only* forty
miles. Well, then. Guess I'd better dirty up my truck if I want
to be taken seriously in these here parts. Scuff up my boots
a bit, too, and maybe stomp on my hat a couple of times."

Her cheeks went a fetching shade of pink. "You are
twisting what I said," she told him, brushing Butterpie
again, her touch gentle but sure. "I meant…"

Tanner envied that little horse. Wished he had a furry
hide, so he'd need brushing, too.

"You *meant* that I'm not a real cowboy," he said. "And

you could be right. I've spent a lot of time on construction sites over the last few years, or in meetings where a hat and boots wouldn't be appropriate. Instead of digging out my old gear, once I decided to take this job, I just bought new."

"I bet you don't even *have* any old gear," she challenged, but she was smiling, albeit cautiously, as though she might withdraw into a disapproving frown at any second.

He took off his hat, extended it to her. "Here," he teased. "Rub that around in the muck until it suits you."

She laughed, and the sound—well, it caused a powerful and wholly unexpected shift inside him. Scared the hell out of him and, paradoxically, made him yearn to hear it again.

* * * * *

Discover how this rugged rancher's wanderlust is tamed in time for a merry Christmas, in
A STONE CREEK CHRISTMAS.
In stores December 2008.

Silhouette®

SPECIAL EDITION™

**FROM *NEW YORK TIMES*
BESTSELLING AUTHOR**

LINDA LAEL MILLER

A STONE CREEK CHRISTMAS

Veterinarian Olivia O'Ballivan finds the animals
in Stone Creek playing Cupid between her and
Tanner Quinn. Even Tanner's daughter, Sophie,
is eager to play matchmaker. With everyone
conspiring against them and the holiday season
fast approaching, Tanner and Olivia may just get
everything they want for Christmas after all!

*Available December 2008
wherever books are sold.*

SPECIAL EDITION™

Kate's Boys

MISTLETOE AND MIRACLES

by *USA TODAY* bestselling author

MARIE FERRARELLA

Child psychologist Trent Marlowe couldn't
believe his eyes when Laurel Greer, the
woman he'd loved and lost, came to him for
help. Now a widow, with a troubled boy who
wouldn't speak, Laurel needed a miracle from
Trent...and a brief detour under the mistletoe
wouldn't hurt, either.

Available in December wherever books are sold.

THE ITALIAN'S BRIDE

Commanded—to be his wife!

Used to the finest food, clothes and women,
these immensely powerful, incredibly
good-looking and undeniably charismatic
men have only one last need: a wife!

They've chosen their bride-to-be and they'll
have her—willing or not!

Enjoy all our fantastic stories in December:

THE ITALIAN BILLIONAIRE'S
SECRET LOVE-CHILD
by CATHY WILLIAMS (Book #33)

SICILIAN MILLIONAIRE,
BOUGHT BRIDE
by CATHERINE SPENCER (Book #34)

BEDDED AND WEDDED FOR REVENGE
by MELANIE MILBURNE (Book #35)

THE ITALIAN'S UNWILLING WIFE
by KATHRYN ROSS (Book #36)

REQUEST YOUR FREE BOOKS!

2 FREE NOVELS PLUS 2 FREE GIFTS!

Silhouette® Desire®

Passionate, Powerful, Provocative!

YES! Please send me 2 FREE Silhouette Desire® novels and my 2 FREE gifts (gifts are worth about $10). After receiving them, if I don't wish to receive any more books, I can return the shipping statement marked "cancel". If I don't cancel, I will receive 6 brand-new novels every month and be billed just $4.05 per book in the U.S. or $4.74 per book in Canada, plus 25¢ shipping and handling per book and applicable taxes, if any*. That's a savings of almost 15% off the cover price! I understand that accepting the 2 free books and gifts places me under no obligation to buy anything. I can always return a shipment and cancel at any time. Even if I never buy another book, the two free books and gifts are mine to keep forever.   225 SDN ERVX 326 SDN ERVM

Name	(PLEASE PRINT)	
Address		Apt. #
City	State/Prov.	Zip/Postal Code

Signature (if under 18, a parent or guardian must sign)

Mail to the **Silhouette Reader Service:**
IN U.S.A.: P.O. Box 1867, Buffalo, NY 14240-1867
IN CANADA: P.O. Box 609, Fort Erie, Ontario L2A 5X3

Not valid to current subscribers of Silhouette Desire books.

Want to try two free books from another line?
Call 1-800-873-8635 or visit www.morefreebooks.com.

* Terms and prices subject to change without notice. N.Y. residents add applicable sales tax. Canadian residents will be charged applicable provincial taxes and GST. Offer not valid in Quebec. This offer is limited to one order per household. All orders subject to approval. Credit or debit balances in a customer's account(s) may be offset by any other outstanding balance owed by or to the customer. Please allow 4 to 6 weeks for delivery. Offer available while quantities last.

Your Privacy: Silhouette Books is committed to protecting your privacy. Our Privacy Policy is available online at www.eHarlequin.com or upon request from the Reader Service. From time to time we make our lists of customers available to reputable third parties who may have a product or service of interest to you. If you would prefer we not share your name and address, please check here. ☐

SDES08R

™ Silhouette®

Desire

COMING NEXT MONTH

#1909 THE BILLIONAIRE IN PENTHOUSE B—
Anna DePalo
Park Avenue Scandals
Who's the mystery man in Penthouse B? She's determined to
uncover his every secret. *He's* determined to get her under his
covers!

#1910 THE TYCOON'S SECRET—Kasey Michaels
Gifts from a Billionaire
He's kept his identity under wraps and hired her to decorate his
billion-dollar mansion. But when seduction turns serious, will the
truth tear them apart?

#1911 QUADE'S BABIES—Brenda Jackson
The Westmorelands
This sexy Westmoreland gets more than he bargained for when he
discovers he's a daddy—times three! Now he's determined to do
the right thing…if she'll have him.…

#1912 THE THROW-AWAY BRIDE—Ann Major
Golden Spurs
A surprise pregnancy and a marriage of convenience brought them
together. Can their newfound love survive the secrets he's been
keeping from her?

#1913 THE DUKE'S NEW YEAR'S RESOLUTION—
Merline Lovelace
Holidays Abroad
Initially stunned by her resemblance to his late wife, the Italian
duke is reluctant to invite her to his villa, but it doesn't take long
for him to invite her into his bed.

#1914 PREGNANCY PROPOSAL—Tessa Radley
The Saxon Brides
She's the girl he's always secretly loved—and is his late brother's
fiancée. When he learns she's pregnant, he proposes—having no
idea she's really carrying *his* baby!

SDCNMBPA1108

Dear Reader,

I adore Manhattan. But then who doesn't? When I was offered the opportunity to work with some of my favorite Desire authors on a series set on Park Avenue, refusing never crossed my mind. The only thing more fun would be taking another trip to New York City—and that is definitely on my agenda.

For a laid-back southern girl there is nothing like the energy of the city that never sleeps. I love visiting places I've seen on TV or in the movies like Times Square, Central Park and Ground Zero to name but a few. I'm sure my practice of smiling at everyone I pass marks me as a tourist, but so what? When I go to Manhattan I'm there to have fun, see the sights and yes, the people, and that brings a smile to my face that I can't smother.

My only regrets: I haven't managed to catch a Broadway play or get to a baseball game on my trips north. So look out New Yorkers. I'll be back and I intend to hit both a Yankees and a Mets game—both just short train rides away—and catch a show or two. Keep your fingers crossed that I don't sing a show tune on the way out of the theater. Trust me, that would be bad.

Emilie

721 SECRETS

*Keeping you up to date on all that goes on
at Manhattan's most elite address!*

Our own Amanda Crawford wins the Dubious Award for Abstinence. She did what no other female New Yorker has ever done—resist TDH (aka tall, dark and handsome) Alex Harper. Once that gorgeous attorney turns on the charm, women normally rush into his arms. But not Amanda. She put the heartthrob hottie through his paces before she succumbed. It's a match made in heaven, sources say. Alex has all the contacts Amanda's fledgling party business needs, and she's the best there is to bring him the publicity he craves. But theirs is more than a business arrangement, according to 721's ninth-floor residents who were kept up all night by their…work.

With Alex's fine pedigree, no doubt Amanda's parents will approve of her man—for the first time ever—but rumor has it she's keeping mum on her love life. How's that possible when she's seeing Manhattan's most eligible bachelor? And just how long will Love 'em and Leave 'em Harper stick around this time? Only time will tell…. Some say we'll know in nine months!